Hector and The Little People

♥

The Little People series is dedicated to 'my little people' who have shown me what love is…Thank you, my children, from this speaker from the heart. I love you all SO much!

♥ Tara Robin Rachel ♥

♥ Troy Ronald Robin ♥

♥ Jacob Jasper ♥

♥ Zack Donald ♥

Hector and The Little People

Hector and The Little People

© 2011 Mary McGillis

This edition was first published in 2011 by

9ᵗʰ Wave Enterprises

Peterborough, Canada

www.MaryMcGillis.com

ISBN: 978-0-9783364-8-6

dear Sasha ♡ & family ♡
Love

Hector

and

TheLittlePeople

and

Mary ♡

Mary McGillis

marymcgillis@live.com

cell: 705-559-3633

Hector and The Little People

♥ *Gratitude is my Attitude* ♥

Thank **YOU** ~ hope you enjoy the Little People journey ~

And now, I thank some of those who have gone before us…

brave souls

Donald Angus McGillis

Catherine Agathe McGillis (Naylen)

John Clare (Jack) Donnelly

Loretta Marie Donnelly (Schuett)

Donald Edward McGillis

Joan Theresa McGillis (Donnelly)

Kelly Ann McGillis

As our ancestors watch over us, always, remember to
give them something to talk about

♥ *thanks* ♥

Table of Contents

Chapter One   *Mary Hickey Meets Hector*   …9

Chapter Two   *Wishing Well*   …33

Chapter Three   *The King and Queen of Faery*   …47

Chapter Four   *Arrival at the Land of Friendship*   …68

Chapter Five   *The Vision of the Three Crosses*   …80

Chapter Six   *Trip to Misty Eyed Falls*   …95

Chapter Seven   *The Gifts from the Four Directions*   …114

Chapter Eight   *Old Mother Shipton's Buried Treasure* …127

Chapter Nine   *Revisiting The Halls of Fame*   …151

Chapter Ten   *The Seven Ls Message*   …162

Chapter Eleven   *Past, Present and Future Meet*   …172

Chapter Twelve   *The Deeps*   …192

Chapter Thirteen   *The Empress*   …203

Chapter Fourteen   *The Day of the Barbecue*   …217

Chapter Fifteen   *Fireworks*   …235

Chapter Sixteen   *The Aftermath*   …248

Chapter Seventeen   *The Final Frontier*   …255

Hector and The Little People

PART ONE

... the story is

Hector and The Little People

Chapter One

Mary Meets Hector

The old man was out of the house and onto the street before his wife reached the front door. The snow was long gone, but the evenings remained cool. She stopped to put on her sweater and pulled at the arms, thinking that it'd better warm up soon because there were only two days left in Spring. She marched down the front steps to see her husband peering down the street. He knew the neighbourhood pretty well and was certain that the alley across the way dead-ended at a high fence. He didn't think the boys had gone down the alley, so they wouldn't be trapped there.

'Boys! I saw you! I saw what you did!' he shouted at the early evening sky. There was no answer except the whistle of the wind through the alley, and something that might have been the desperate breathing of trapped children. His wife stood beside him with her arms planted on her hips.

'All the Saints in Heaven! You'll catch your death if you don't get back in the house. Look at you with a t-shirt and stocking feet!' She took one look out onto High Street before turning on her heels and heading inside for the phone. She had watched Thor, Tom and Angus Hickey darting across her neighbours' lawns and she knew she must phone the police. She did not hesitate as she spoke:

'Police? Yes, I'd like to report some mischief.'

Somehow, even though there were 70,000 other people in Lakeville, the dispatcher knew the voice of his favorite busybody. Her reputation as a nosey neighbour was legend, as were her calls to the Lakeville Community Police Department. She liked the Hickey family, but ignored her husband's objections as she offered names and addresses to the dispatcher. The boys were up to no good and she would teach them a lesson.

I've heard of nerve before. Why just last summer someone stole the seven dwarfs right off the front porch next door. Up and gone. That porch was too damn big for any good anyway. Why she ever had such a porch built, I'll never know. But this neighbourhood is going to the dogs. Almost every night there's some kind of commotion in someone's yard. And people roaming around all hours of the day and night. You'd think we live in a big metropolis with all the gangs and such. Drugs, too. At least their oldest child is a good girl. What's her name again? Ruby. Yes, she's a good girl. Well, her brothers won't be getting away with anything when I'm on watch.

Outside, the boys were in the alley talking in hushe
tones after the old man went back into his house to join his
wife: 'Good. I think she's on the phone now, probably telling
all her friends about the excitement. How many does that
make Angus?' Thor asked his eight-year-old brother.

'50,' said Angus.

'Seriously? I never thought there were so many
gnomes in the whole city!'
year,' said Tom. 'Maybe we should go into the gnome
business, Thor.'

'Awesome idea! Let's get out of here.' Even at his
young age, Thor trusted Angus' math; and Tom was a genius
with numbers who was known to everyone as 'Money Man'.
It didn't surprise Thor that Tom noticed stuff like new
gnomes. All three boys were quite the little entrepreneurs.

They heard the wailing police cars when they were
halfway up High Street, but the sound of the far off sirens did
not dampen their spirits or even register as threatening. Thor
was in his third year of a paper route and even though not all
neighbours got his paper, he delivered weekly flyers to every
home. The old man was just trying to scare them. And she
always had a big smile for him. And besides, there's no way
they saw the gnome. Thor pulled his sweater around his face.
The boys were anxious to finish their daunting task, as the
biting wind seemed fiercer when they climbed the steep hill.

They arrived under the water tower with the last of their loot and the full moon passed from behind a cloud bathing them and their ill-gotten friends in bright moonlight. The gnomes stood shortly, portly and in an Easter Island like circle around Lakeville's largest advertising board. The city's name could be seen for miles because of the height of the letters and the height of the tower. Once Thor completed the circle with the 50th gnome, he was in a big hurry to get back home because they had promised their mother they'd be home before dark. The glow of the moonlight had startled him.

Meanwhile, at the Hickey residence, the doorbell rang. When Mary opened the door to two uniformed police officers, a look of shock registered on her face. The tall and obviously younger policeman said, 'Good evening, Mrs. Hickey; we're here to talk to your boys.'

'Oh, my. They're over a street playing road hockey, but they said they'd be home by dark. Has something happened?' she said.

The older, stout policeman said, 'Ma'am, one of the neighbours said they saw three children that looked like your children stealing garden gnomes tonight.'

'Garden gnomes? *Ha. There must be some mistake. And why would kids steal garden gnomes?*' As she was talking and thinking, she thought of her three boys. She never worried about the two younger boys playing outside, especially when Thor was with them. Even though they had their moments where you swear they'd kill each other, all of the boys were kind and well loved in the neighbourhood. Thor prided himself on knowing the names of every neighbour on the street, probably because he was the top school fundraiser for any of their campaigns. Tom and Angus were two peas in a pod, fun loving and full of life. She saw the boys coming up the driveway and her voice faltered. She remembered the dinner conversation a few days earlier. She had served tap water and one of the boys had commented on the rusty, metallic aftertaste and her comment came back to haunt her. *'Somebody better find 50 gnomes and circle that water tower on High Street. Nothing but magic will help Lakeville now!'*

The next day, the newspaper delivery man brought Thor's papers right on time. Mary had prayed that the incident would go unreported, but there on the front page was the headline and story: *'Are You Missing Any Gnomes?'* Her heart sank.

'Police discovered a stockpile of stolen garden gnomes last night, all of them neatly circling the Lakeville Water Tower on High Street. Most of the 50 gnomes, of various sizes, shapes and forms were stolen from the Newton Park area and east of Hennessey Street. Some of the gnomes have already been returned to their owners. "We have had in previous summers incidents like this and it's usually kids

doing a prank. They'll go around a particular neighbourhood and round up a bunch of these from different lawns then dump them in a certain location and we end up with a whole pile of them," said Sgt. Shaughnessy. "This incident is a little different in that the gnomes were all found standing in a circle and summer hasn't yet begun." Twenty-seven gnomes have yet to be claimed. Call 555-1122 Ext 555 if you're missing one.'

Mary was so relieved that no mention of her boys was included that she let out an audible sigh of relief. She knew her 16-year-old daughter, Ruby, would have been distraught seeing 'her boys' names in the paper, not to mention livid for what they'd done. Luckily, Ruby had stayed the night at her best friend's house and didn't know anything about the gnomes or the police visit, giving Mary time to settle down. Although Ruby looked like a younger version of Mary, she was more of a disciplinarian and taskmaster than her mother. She was an award-winning scholar and, wise beyond her years, knew her purpose in life. Her many successes intimidated the boys and filled her mother and father with awe. Mary sat up straight in her chair. *And I haven't even called their father yet!*

'Mom! There's a man with a funny looking hat coming up the driveway,' said Tom.

'Is he coming here or next door?' she said as she stood up to check. *What now?* It'd be nice if Royal were home when the kaka hit the fan for once. Somehow, he always managed to be on tour when major stuff went down. Luck 'o the Irish. Ruby was lucky her Dad did go out of the country; otherwise she'd never get to overnight at her friends, let alone have a party! But Royal had missed so much of their growing years, too. When he was in town he was often out at rehearsals or management meetings, so they often talked to him more when he was touring. At least there he only had to perform and sightsee. Maybe they'd go for a trip to visit him on the last leg of the European tour.

'Here. He's at the door," Tom said as the doorbell rang.

'Don't open it; I will,' said Mary.

Thinking it would be a salesman, she almost gasped as she looked down at the little man standing on her stoop. It wasn't his size, really. It was more his clothes that shocked her. She thought back to her childhood when her babysitter, Molly MacInnerney, told her the tales from long ago. Molly, God rest her soul, could tell a story like no other. Her Gaelic accent was heavy, but she weaved stories from the legends she'd heard as a wee lass on the moors. Her face crinkled into a thousand creases as she smiled, her eyes glistened with mischievousness. How could her four-foot-eight frame possibly hold what must have been the biggest heart in the world? Mary had always loved being compared to Molly.

Although she was a foot taller, Mary's lush auburn hair and Irish complexion matched Molly to a 't'. Mary also liked to think she had turned out kind and sweet like her old friend, too. Molly always brought favourite candies, like Smarties, but it was the stories that everyone loved so much.

She said there was a time of giants, or maybe gods, and unicorns and dragons. She said it was real. The Tuatha Dé Danann were giants that lived in a world of love, peace and joy. The Formorians, where had they come from? The Formorians were the bad guys and they'd wreaked havoc on the love world, warring with anyone who stood in the way of their progress and greed. The giants had gone underground, Molly said, and became the wee folk of Celtic legends. The wee folk flourished underground and vowed never to return to the badlands or live in a land without love. Molly said she visited the wee folk right up until she died at 102, several years before. The visitor standing on the porch looked like he could be Molly McInnerney's twin brother.

'Hello, Ma'am. I am from the P.L.A.C.E. and need to talk to you about the gnome incident. I know your thirteen-year-old boy, Thor Franklin Hickey, and his two younger brothers, as accomplices, were involved. May I come in please?' he said rather seriously.

She regained her composure and said, 'Did you say you were from the police, sir?'

'No, Ma'am. I said I am from the P.L.A.C.E.'

'What place?'

'The People of Little Association of Canadians Everywhere.'

'I don't understand.'

'Ma'am, I will explain everything to you, if you would only invite me in.'

What had Molly said about inviting in the wee folk? *God and Molly, help us now.* Not wanting to be rude to such an odd, but non-threatening looking fellow, Mary decided to invite him in. Mary may have invited him in because of his familiarity, in that he looked like Molly, or because of her innate sense of adventure, or possibly because of he was using some kind of Faerykind mind control. Whatever the case, she had to hear his story. 'Certainly, come in, come in,' and when she backed up a step to let him enter, she stumbled over Angus and Tom who had gone unnoticed behind her.

'Angus, be careful. Here, let Mr.', her voice trailed off.

'Oh, I think Angus can guess my name,' said the odd looking little man.

Everyone giggled because his hair was a mass of matted ringlets, quite long and capped with a dark green silken toque. The dark green was also one of the predominant shades of the dozens of shades of green in his shirt, jacket, pants and shoes. It crossed her mind that Tom could've said 'the man in green' or 'hairy' or something worse, but she leaned toward Mr. Green since the color did stand out on the fellow that she'd just invited into their home.

'Hairy! Harry!' Angus and Tom yelled in unison.

'Nope. The name's Hector, boys. I knew you'd say Harry, though," Hector laughed.

'Would you like a cup of tea or a glass of water?' said Mary, suddenly and inexplicably feeling totally comfortable with her decision to invite this strange man into their home.

'Oh, that's kind of you to offer, Mrs. Hickey, but I'd prefer a wee pint, if you have one,' said Hector.

'What's a pint, Mr. Hector?' asked Tom. None of the boys had a shy bone in their bodies, but Tom had always been more upfront and in your face than the others.

'It's the nectar of the little people, Tom; keeps our bones and minds healthy.'

'Can we have one, too, Mom?' asked Angus. He was such a doll; Mary had to touch the top of his head and smile at him.

'Actually, I do have a six-pack of Corona in the root cellar. I keep it in case company drops in Hector. Do you like Corona?'

'Especially with a wee slice of lime, Mrs. Hickey.'

'Please call me Mary, Hector, and yes, I have a lime.'

Tom said, 'Oh. You mean beer. I'll get it Mom. Angus, we can't have any, can we Mom?' Tom was calling as he ran down the stairs to the basement.

'Not today, Tommy.'

'Come and sit in the living room, Hector.'

'Oh, I'd prefer the coziness of the sunroom, Mrs. Hickey, I mean Mary.'

'Hey, how did you know Tom's name and how did you know about the sunroom?' Mary's comfort level dropped drastically and alarm showed in her voice and she stopped in her tracks.

'It's okay, Mary. I know you're a little confused, no pun intended, by all of this stuff, but that's why I'm here as the ambassador to explain.'

'The ambassador?'

'Ah, yes, Mary. The little people have decided to rekindle our friendship with your people. It's been hundreds of years since we went underground, so to speak, and we think it's time to rekindle our friendship again.'

'Again?'

'Don't you remember the North American legends and the Celtic legends about the wee folk for goodness sake?' Tom appeared, holding a beer, and said, 'He means leprechauns, Ma.'

'Well, most of the 'Cauns live across the pond, but we have a fair share here in the settlement up near Ottawa. It's more of the gnomes and brownies that settled here in Lakeville. Sometimes we host parties in your backyard and that's how I know about the sunroom. Remember coming out one night awhile back to see why your sensor lights kept coming on?'

Mary well remembered that night. Royal had just left for his tour and she and Ruby had been playing cribbage at the dining room table. The noises coming from their backyard were not subtle. Someone or some THING was out there, partying. She was too afraid to check out the sound and light show by herself and it had taken her awhile to cajole her Ruby into exploring the strange goings on. The back sunroom door led out onto a small landing with stairs going down either side of the gardens. As Mary and Ruby stepped onto the landing, the floodlights went on. The thirty-foot cedar hedges blocked everything but the starry sky above and the lights cast long shadows of the crabapple tree to the edges of the yard. The strange rustling sounds heard in the stillness of the night surrounded them, right there beside them even, yet there was nothing to be seen. Together, they walked down the one set of stairs and directly out to the tree.

'If you were there, Hector, I couldn't see you, but you would've seen Ruby and me running real fast back to the sunroom.'

'Yes, we all had a good laugh. Sorry, but you are funny; throwing your arms up like that and all.'

'Hector, probably a stupid question, but how did you know about the boys and the gnomes?' Mary had an ever growing understanding that something magical was afoot.

21

Hector giggled and his eyes shone with merriment. 'Mary, Mary. We're with your boys '24/7', as they say, when they're playing outside. Crazy worlds out there, you know. The Queen had been teetering about reconnecting with you Earthen folk, but when she heard about the Hickey boys, that cemented her resolve.'

'Earthen folk? Queen?'
Angus and Tom were only eight and nine respectively and Thor was barely thirteen, but they knew something life-changing was happening and sat quietly on the dark maroon leather couch. Mary shifted uncomfortably on the matching stool and Hector jumped up from his roost on the big, comfy chair.

'Questions, questions. They'll all be answered in good time, but my purpose today is to elicit your aid in retrieving our 27 gnome friends from your police station!'

'Oh my. The police were wonderful about the whole incident after they learned about the ridiculous reason. Thank God they didn't charge the boys and all. And kept their names from the newspaper,' said Mary.

'Precisely why you are the perfect candidate to help our friends without further magic being involved at this time. The Queen was quite adamant about that,' Hector said.

'How could I? What do you mean? What Queen? Does she own the gnomes?'

'Ha. You are as funny as funny can be, Mary. How can a soul ask four questions in one breath? It must be a world record,' said Hector. 'You are my human decoy and I mean that those gnomes are my friends and they are loyal subjects of the Faery Realm. However, here in the Mary Realm, they aren't normally seen. Now that they've been captured by your boys, ugh, we have to collect them, bring them back here and they'll be returned to their normal un-stone state!'

'Oh my goodness. You make this sound sane, Hector. If this is real and not a dream, why would the police give the gnomes back to the family that stole them for goodness sake?' said Mary.

'I know, I know!' said Angus. 'We can say that we'll return them to their owners, Ma.'

'And out of the mouths of babes, Mother,' said Hector.

'Oh, Hector, they'll never go for that,' said Mary.

'Oh, Hector, they'll never go for that,' said Hector, mimicking Mary's voice, inflections and all. Hector went on to explain that he had a powerful and persuasive voice and absolutely would not resort to the use of magic, unless necessary.

As the boys rolled on the ground laughing, Hector finished his Corona and said, "Mary, Mary. I'll have that lime next time. And just so you know, I have a few tricks up my sleeve. I want you to play decoy for today, so you can see how a gnome works firsthand. You know, I'm your Uncle Hector on your Ma's side, come to help out,' said Hector. 'You're my limousine, Mary. Should you agree, of course.'

For a moment, all eyes were on Mary.

'Well, I'd love to help out the wee folk. You, too, boys?' said Mary. *What in the world am I saying?*

'Yippee yi yay! Hooray! Yes!' they yelled whole-heartedly.

'BUT...' and they all looked at Mary...

'I don't think we can legally fit 27 gnomes in the van!' said Mary.

'Ha. Mary, you are funny, funny. And you are absolutely right. I will rent a large limousine van and we will all travel together,' said Hector.

Hector had insisted on driving her van and she refused the offer. After all, he had just drank a beer and at his size, that would have had some effect.

'I don't mean to sound crass, but are you tall enough to drive a regular van?' asked Mary.

'Mary, you are crass. And no, I'm not," said Hector, snatching the keys from her hand and looking directly at Mary. Her intuitiveness, which Mary had always trusted completely, told her that this gnome was no ordinary being and to allow him command of the situation.

If Mary hadn't seen all the normal landmarks on the way down Hunter Street, she would've sworn the van had flown to the rental store. And when the boys were thirsty, he magically pulled a six-pack of their favourite drink out from under his seat. Mary had cleaned out her 'Bessy van' the day before and she was positive that there was nothing under any of the seats.

It was business as usual and the salesclerk at the car rental depot didn't blink an eye at Hector.

'You were lucky to get this limo van, Mr. Grodstooth,' said the clerk as he handed Hector back his driver's licence and credit card. 'It just came back in this morning, earlier than expected.'

'Luck 'o the Irish,' said Hector with a wink. 'We'll have it back sooner than you expect, too, I expect.'

The clerk looked at him and smiled.

'Doesn't matter if you're early back, same price. If you have it back after three tomorrow, though, we'll have to charge you for another day,' he said. 'Here are the keys and please follow me. We'll get you going now.'

I can't believe that guy doesn't think Hector is strange. Maybe he's being polite.

'No, Mary. He's seeing me as I want him to see me. Mr. Hector Grodstooth, average guy.'

'You can read minds?' said Mary. *Of course the little booger can! Look at what has transpired in the last hour.*

'Now, Mary. Nothing that wouldn't come out of the mouth of a goddess shall pass your lips. Or is that 'lips that touch liquor will never touch mine'?' said Hector.

Hanging out with a gnome is a pleasure. He's so funny and I like the way the lights turn green so fast.

'That's more like it, something truly worthy of coming out of the lips of creation,' Hector said as the clerk wrote down the odometer and had Hector initial it. He didn't say it aloud, but Mary heard him as clear as a bell. She turned to see if her boys had heard him and saw them fighting over seat rights in the back of the limo. Hector climbed in with them and magically they quietened down.

"Wow, that was fast. Please tell me your tricks!' said Mary.

'Oh, it was nothing. I thought they might enjoy a fancy chocolate shake, Mother Mary, and I was right. Happy as larks they are, I'm sure. Now, it's off to work we go,' said Hector as they got into the van.

Hector took the time alone to explain a few gnome views, considering she was about to meet 27 of the finest. There was one 'in charge' of her household, but when Ruby came along, the Queen insisted on their daughter having her own gnome as a permanent guardian.

'Yes, like a guardian angel,' Hector chuckled. 'Except more in the physical realm, you know, the Mary Realm.'

'You have a funny way with words, Hector.'

'Ah, I was taught by the best. My surrogate mother was none other than Elizabeth Loretta Grodstooth, Master of Light,' said Hector.

'What a beautiful title,' said Mary.

Hector thought about his Bezzy for a second. He missed her so. Not many of the wee folk even knew her real name, and here he was telling it to a human. Not a real human, though. Well, she was real enough, just that she had so much wee folk blood in her bloodline that it was foolhardy not to think that she'd remember someday. The humans called them halfbreeds, Metis and the like, but the wee folk honoured the sacredness of bloodmingling. The humans chose to be scared; the wee folk chose to be sacred.

'What a beautiful being,' said Hector. 'I digress. When we get inside, I'd like you to do the talking, if you please. Like we planned, short and sweet. And then we'll be off,' Hector said as they pulled up in front of the police station. He couldn't let the thoughts of Bezzy distract him from this task. The Queen was livid about the Hickey incident and he knew that time was short. He'd tell Mary about Bezzy another time.

The longest part of the day was having the police help to load all the gnomes into the limousine van. After the thanks and apologies all around, Mary wanted the boys to sit in the front with her for the drive home. Of course, they wouldn't hear of it. She was amazed by Hector, but if these gnomes were really coming to life, that means there'd be 27 other little beings with her boys. Hector tried to calm Mary:

'Please do not think like that, Mary. The boys will be fine. In fact, they're about to meet their gnome protectors, and there's not much finer than that,' Hector said.

'I'd like to be there when that happens,' said Mary.

'OK, Mary. I'll tell you what. We'll wait until we're safely in your garage and then I'll help them back and then they can march their own little behinds through your side door because I think they've had enough man or woman handling for one day and we'll have a tea party to thank you. I insist,' said Hector.

Hector's plan calmed Mary and they had a swift, enjoyable return ride home. Mary always loved coming around the bend from downtown and seeing the lake. Somehow the water soothed her.

'Did you know that the fountain has been in Wee Lake since the seventies, Hector,' said Mary.

'Aye, Mary. Did you know that 2000 Irish settlers came here in the 1800s and started this town with the help of the local natives and little people?' said Hector.

'Hector, of course I know about the settlers. So many were quarantined because of typhoid fever right here. So many died. And the truth about the Indigenous peoples is starting to come out now, about how much they helped. But

I never heard talk about the little people, other than some legends about them being in the woods out near the reservation. Not here in town, though,' said Mary.

'Our finest healers were here, working together day and night. They were tough times, and even though many died, many more were saved,' said Hector.

'It sounds as if you were here,' said Mary.

'Oh, here we are! Marvellousness abounds!' said Hector.

As they turned into her driveway, Mary came back to the present day and noticed the paint peeling off the garage door. *How embarrassing. I've got to get that painted.* She was thankful that the white brick didn't need upkeep. *What on Earth am I going to serve?* She certainly didn't have enough Corona, but Hector had said 'tea party' anyway. But she didn't have enough cups for everyone to drink at the same time. She was about to say so to Hector as he opened the back door of the limo. Little did Mary know that this would be one of the last times she would worry about the mundane tasks in life.

'Please allow me to introduce the Hickey boys to our gnome representatives. Come out of there boys… There. And now, everyone file out, one at a time, no pushing, Tommy. Please, let's go to the sunroom for the feast and we'll have our friends come in and join us for further introductions!' said Hector.

Mary led the way. She walked up the three steps to the side door in the garage and turned her old doorknob as she had thousands of times before. She let out an audible gasp as she opened the door to a new life. The boys ran around her as she stopped.

'Way cool, Mom!'

'WHAT!'

'This is our house?'

The boys ran through the kitchen yelling to each other.

'Hector,' was all Mary could muster.

Without even entering the house, she could see that it had been transformed into a festive setting, with balloons and streamers and decorations everywhere. Impossibly, the rooms were larger, yet the house looked the same when they drove up. As she slowly walked in, she saw the little bathroom off

the kitchen, was not a little bathroom anymore. Coming into the house through the garage door and up a few stairs, more often than not the bathroom door would be ajar, the plain oak vanity with the sink peeking out. All of that had disappeared. Mary saw the new arched door open to a winter wonderland scene. Her blue and yellow décor gone, the room had ballooned into a montage of silvers, golds and the whitest whites. *Just what the kids need. What am I saying? It's my dreams and desires bathroom. But what happened to my blue*

30

and yellow bathroom? This is impossible. Hector. Mary didn't realize she'd said his name aloud. She was busy taking in the double bowl sink, mirrors trimmed with what looked to be real gold like all of the taps and hardware. *Pure white hand towels monogrammed and embossed in gold! They will last! Too funny.*

Hector came up beside her and said: 'Yes, Mary. I know about your limited worldview. You see things in terms of what you dream about, what you desire and what you think you need. You have lists and categorizing down to a fine art. The Little People have decided it's time you expand your horizons, stretch your imagination, ah... a little at least... so come, I'll take you on a grand tour of your new Hector home. Sounds like the kids like it,' said Hector.

'Hector it isn't even the colours. It's the marble. It's the gold. It's spectacular. It can't be real,' said Mary as she walked up the stairs. She glanced to her left and was visibly shaken.

'Oh, my. The kitchen. I mean. Where is the the kitchen?'

'Mom! I love it! How did Hector do this? He's the best magical leprechaun I ever met,' said Angus running by them to the fridge. 'I knew it. It's full, Ma!' Tom and Thor ran past to look, too.

'Better stuff in the living room and sunroom, though,' said Thor.

'And the fountain, Hector, can we drink that stuff?' said Angus.

'Fountain?' Mary said.

'Yes, Angus, and yes, Mary.'

The kitchen was a replica of what Mary had cut and pasted onto her dreamboard. She had Ruby and the boys help her cut out pictures from all the lifestyle magazines and together they'd created a fantasy home. Hector began walking her through her own creation. *She had to pinch herself. Ouch. Not dreaming. What is this?* The kitchen had been transformed into a 40 by 40 foot room from a very small 18 by 12 footer. *Geez. Grandma always said don't wish too hard for something or you might just get it. It'll take ages just to mop this floor. Jumpin' Joe. It's marble. I don't even know how to clean it. Oh, I love that island. It looks even better in real life.*

The countertops were marble, too. And there was a doublestove with no burners. She loved the faucet. *It's one of those three foot faucets that have the spray gun, the tap and the water drinking spout. Those boys better not fight with that gun! Ruby'll love it.* Hector was holding her hand, leading her into the livingroom. *How can I breathe?* The living room now featured a working fireplace. She didn't notice the roaring fire at first, mainly because of the size of the snowy pillars and the serene whiteness of the room.

'No time to dawdle,' Hector said as they walked toward the back of the house. He turned to look at Mary as they stood at the doorway. The sign draped across the floor to ceiling picture windows said: *Welcome to Mary's Realm.*

Chapter 2

The Wishing Well

The twenty-seven gnomes entered the Hickey residence in what seemed an endless line of little people smiling and dancing about. It was by no means an orderly procession, but an obvious celebration. The three protectors immediately went to introduce themselves to each of the Hickey boys when Hector called everyone to attention. Snelton had been longest with the Queen's Company, the name for the gnomes who staffed at *Castle Lyonstyme* and, accordingly, was awarded the coveted position of being Protector to the eldest son, Thor.

The order of birth meant nothing in the world of little folk, as they had a remembering about the time before and knew that everyone carried all lifetimes within them. Yet Snelton's people had a special fondness for the oldest boy, Thor, as his birth had been foretold. It was a great honour to Snelton that he was chosen as the guardian. When Thor came into the world screaming at the stroke of midnight, during a thunderstorm to boot, everyone in the land of Faery took notice. Afterward, when it was confirmed that he had the cherry tattoo on his backside cheek, the Queen had intervened and assigned Snelton. In the land of Faery, Queen

Titiana had been unsure with Ruby, but when Thor arrived, she knew the time foretold by the seers and the seekers had come. On Earth, Mary had assured Royal that all would be fine for a home birth, as all had gone so well with Ruby's birth four years prior. Everything was happening on schedule, right up until the lights went out. She soon found out that with all the new technology, the electric world comes to a halt when you can't plug anything in. 'Thank God for Nikola Tesla' was one of her favourite axioms. Mary had been calming herself with some classical music when the music stopped. Ruby, like any frightened three-year-old, started with the questions. *Mama, are you okay? Mama, is the baby okay? Mama, is God mad? Is She?*

Startled back to the present time by Hector's booming voice, Mary left the bedroom of 13 years ago and returned to the present of Hector in her home.

'I am happy you're all back in one piece, my wee friends; thanks so much Mary and family. And now, I'd like everyone to get some treats and take their special seats and hear my plan,' said Hector.

Despite his small stature, Mary saw that Hector was a commanding presence. In the transformed room, there were seats for every single gnome and special chairs with names on them for the Hickey family. The picture windows overlooked their secluded yard, but little else remained the same. Mary smiled as she sat in her chair, Goddess Mary emblazoned in gold. *So much gold. I wonder what it means?* The balloons and ribbons were all gold and white, except for the rainbow trees of helium balloons all over the house. The background music sounded familiar somehow, but Mary didn't recognize the band. *Happy music makes for a happy home. That's what Royal always says. Ah. Music. Oh. Royal. What will Royal say?* Mary had left him a message earlier, but hadn't heard back from him yet.

'Order, order,' said Hector. 'There'll be lots of time to talk after I finish, folks. Thank you, thank you. First off, I want to start by telling you about a sign. There's a small sign in the back of a wee church in Ireland that reads: 'God smiles when people make plans'. A direct quote, I'm sure. However, folks, I am not people. I am Ambassador Hector Grodstooth, Special Emissary to The One. Truer words were never spake. All of you in this room are from this moment on, Assistants to The One, and shall forevermore be known as such. For example, my friend Mary here, your work will be particularly important in light of the Earth changes we are experiencing now. I have printed individual assignments on my special Goldlink paper. As some of you know, the words are visible only to the Royal Family and to the being it is intended for, no others. I expect to be in the general vicinity for some time, and I am trying to cover all bases, but you all know that you can reach me anytime you want by express thought. I'm sure you know me well enough by now, Mary and boys, to know what I mean. And you know I mean what I say and I say what I mean. By the way, in all our rush, I forgot to mention about your daughter. I've sent her on ahead to greet the Queen.'

Ruby? What?

'Don't worry, Mary. She's in the best of hands.'

Mary managed a weak smile. Hadn't he said the Queen was livid?

Christ above her, Christ below her, Christ to the left, Christ to the right, Christ surround her.

The old St. Patrick's Hymn comforted Mary. Whenever she invoked these words around anyone, she knew they'd be protected.

What is he talking about now?

'In summing up, yes, I am about to sum up, Mary; I want to first thank you for the work you have done and for what you are about to do. And remember, my kinfolk, teach your children well. As you will see in your instructions, we are to share the magical possessions only after the wishing well has been established,' Hector said.

Mary's eyes followed Hector's glance to the right and she saw an old, unpainted wooden crate sitting near her desk. It was about a foot high and a couple long, and the faded words 'WISHING WELL' were stamped in blue ink on the side facing her. She could see it was empty.

What did he say? Magical possessions?

'OK, OK. I said we will talk about the magical possessions after the ground rules are laid out for this wishing well.'

'That well, there, Hector?' said Mary, pointing to the crate.

'Yes. It may look like an old crate for bananas, but when you know about the magic, it's almost as good as the word abracadabra, which happens to be the best magical word ever invented! Knowing it works when you step one of your feet into it is the key. You know, ask and ye shall receive, folks. Who wants to go first?'

Several gnomes ran and pushed a little, vying for the spot closest to the well.

'OK, Snelton, you first,' said Hector.

'Thor, up here now.'

Mary wondered what in the world was going through her children's minds. She lightened up visibly when she saw the excitement in Thor's eyes. He had his father's eyes, brown and warm with long lashes. He expected to grow taller than his mother over the winter and equated his physical stature with independence. Neither of his parents had complained when he had his long curls cut off and his hair spiked the month before.

'Do I get to make a wish?' asked Thor.

'Thor Hickey, you are the wish. Remember your Mama telling you: 'Don't wish too hard for something or ye just might get it?'' This here wishing well is a gift for your family from the little people. You may get what you think you desire, but this well is a learning tool so you can figure out what you truly desire.'

'I truly desire a new set of Tama drums, baby blue if you have any in stock,' said Thor.

'Hey. Do I have any say in my house?" said Mary.

'Relax Mama Mary; your turn will come. We are trying to illustrate a quick point while all are gathered.'

'Ah. That explains everything. Not,' said Mary.

'OK, Thor, come to the well. There. If you have one foot planted firmly in Mary's Realm and one foot planted in the Well, you'll have whatever it 'tis you're a wishin' for. Now remember, I said firmly, meaning you have to be aware of where your feet are. It won't work for you if both feet are in the Mary Realm,' said Hector.

'What if we put both feet in the Wishing Well?' asked Angus.

'And I knew it'd be you asking that question, Angus. The answer is simple. You'd be gone. Gone from Mary's Realm till I care to come and collect your backside from the Queen's old dungeon. And that dungeon hasn't been used in centuries, so I don't even know what's there anymore. Don't be planting both your feet there, Hickey clan.'

There was much hullabaloo coming from the living room, as the gnomes had turned to see the sparkling set of baby blue drums there.

'Thor, your wish?' said Hector.

'Hector, I love you,' said Thor, blowing a kiss to the grand gnome as he ran to the drums.

'I want a turn,' said Tom.

'No, it's my turn; I'm the youngest,' said Angus.

'Stop. They're here for good, boys, or at least until your Mama gets her wish. Thor, back here, now,' said Hector.

'I'm a good boy,' said Angus.

'No, I said for good, for keeps,' said Hector.

'Can I have a turn,' said Tom.

'Me, too,' said Angus.

'OK, OK. I see what you mean, Mama. But here's how it'll be. Your protectors have to be with you young 'uns for the first four wishes. By then, you'll get the gist. So, Granno and Jumper, you come and get to work with Tom and Angus. I'd like to see the others in the drum room, I mean, Mary's living room. Tut, tut,' said Hector.

'Very funny, Hector. He can keep them, but they'll have to go in the garage or basement,' said Mary.

'They can't go in the garage because the moisture will warp them, Ma,' said Thor.

40

'Maybe the wishing well will put an un-warp spell on them for you,' said Mary.

As they entered the living room, Mary stopped mid sentence. She hadn't noticed the grand staircase when they rushed into the sunroom.

How did I not notice that?

Replacing the carpeted, circular staircase was a much larger and grander, sweeping stairs. The standard spindles had been transformed into gold and white spirals, circling this way and that. The stairs looked like a work of art, with a new white banister, also embossed with gold. The chandelier was stunning. What looked to be four white lotus flowers were encircled by hundreds of pink and purple stained glass flowers, shimmering in the light.

'Ah, you like your stairs, Mary?' said Hector. 'You'll be noticing many things in here for weeks on end, things you've thunk into existence. Your shopping list of desires was a wee bit longer than your shopping list of needs.'

As Hector was speaking, Mary noticed the new floor to ceiling drapes in the dining room. Their gold-flecked deep mauve colour complemented the grandeur of the maroon leather chairs and the mahogany round table.

Such wide chairs and so many. Twelve. Guess he doesn't know that it's only for our kids and us.

'Yes, Mary, I do know that. It has been written,' said Hector.

'Oh, Hector. You creep me out when you do that. If you'd let me finish thinking, I was thinking it's a great party spot now. I'll bet we could sit two, maybe three gnomes on one of those chairs,' said Mary.

'Crass, but practical, that's our Mary,' said Hector.

'I especially love the alcove dining experience. Look at those windows and that chandelier. I see they're almost identical. I don't remember ever seeing a picture of those, Hector,' said Mary.

'Actually, those are a favourite of mine from the Queen's Knowth home, replicated of course. I thought you'd enjoy the grandeur, seemed in keeping with your sense of style,' said Hector.

Laughing and ooing and ahhing filled the room. Mary turned to see a puppy running across the room.

'Hector, don't tell me they can make things come to life?' said Mary.

'Ha. No, no. We leave that kind of creating up to the Creator. These puppies are what you call Irish Wolf Hounds, gifts from the King and Queen.'

'Puppies?'

As she asked, another puppy ran out from the back.

'Yes, Mary. The puppies will be great for protection and for companionship. We have to keep you out of worry. You'll know your children are safe with these fellows on guard.'

42

'Aren't they huge when full grown?' said Mary

'Yes, Ma'am. Like a horse to me,' said Hector.

'When anyone wants to walk them or let them run, they put one foot in the Well and say so; instantly, they'll all be transported to a corner of the world for playing outside.'

'I wish Royal were here. I wish Ruby were here,' said Mary.

'Try the well out, Mary,' said Hector.

'Seriously?'

'Come on. I should have told you this already. So much to teach,' said Hector.

As she was walking back to the well, the boys were dragging at her arms.

'Can we keep them, Ma? Can we keep them?'

It was surreal. There were so many little people. And Hector.

When we were little, didn't my sister tell me not to think about the wee folk? No good would come of it, she'd said.

'Mary, Mary. I know you're overwhelmed. Put your foot there. Now make the wish.'

What was I wishing? Oh ya, Royal. Royal, I wish you were here, now.'

'Mary? What? Is that you? Where are you?' said Royal.

Royal's 3-D image appeared in the very air in front of Mary. It was like a movie, but no projector was there. Just Royal. He was shaving off his five o'clock shadow.

She started to cry.

What is going on? Am I dreaming?

'Dad, we got dogs! Dad! We got dogs!' yelled Tom and Angus.

'And Tama drums, Dad,' said Thor.

'Royal, you can come home right now and you can return the same way, only if you agree,' said Hector.

'Home? How? What? Yes, I want to,' said Royal.

As he said 'Yes', he was moved into the sunroom and finished his sentence there, in his home.

'Who are you?' Royal asked Hector.

'I am the Ambassador of the Little People. We have come to rekindle our friendship with humankind and have asked your family to help with this assignment,' said Hector.

'Wow. Mary, are you OK?' said Royal, putting his arms around her waist. Without waiting for an answer, he looked around and did a head count and said, 'And where's Ruby?'

'She's with the Queen, Dad. She's with the Queen.'

'Queen? Where?'

"I see it's time for us to meet the King and Queen,' said Hector, pulling an amethyst amulet necklace out from under his shirt. As he did so, the Queen appeared, asking 'Hector?'

'Your Excellency. As you can see, we're gathered here enjoying your Wishing Well and puppies,' said Hector.

'Excellent,' the Queen said, broadening the band so everyone could see Ruby.

'Hi Mom. Dad. Everyone!' Ruby said with a growing smile.

'Let's join them now, Ruby. The King will come when he returns,' said The Queen.

'OK,' said Ruby.

With that, the Queen and Ruby appeared beside the Well. Titiana looked regal in a deep purple robe, trimmed with white fur and golds and bestudded with jewels of every kind and colour. Ruby had grown to a 5' 10" height before high school and towered over the Queen. The golden highlights in her brown hair matched the Queen's colouring and though the two were oddly matched in size, they seemed a likely pair. When Ruby had returned home from her overnight at her friend's house, she had found the Queen in full regalia sitting in her living room. Ruby had long suspected that she had faery blood and had insisted to her Mama that she must, too. She wasn't afraid when the Queen rose from the chair; she was thrilled to make contact. Many nights she had seen something out of the corner of her eye or heard her name whispered, but it was always a fleeting glimpse of a world she longed to know. She had dropped her overnight bag near the stairs and walked over to kneel before her Queen. Anyone looking into the room would have noticed that the young girl bore a striking resemblance to Titiana. They had the same straight nose and flared nostrils that suggested character traits like persistence and determination. Their chins jutted out ever so slightly, adding courage and bravery to their strength of character. It was the eyes that showed the connection, though. Titiana's blue eyes were as clear as rainwater. The only difference was that Ruby's eyes had flecks of gold, somehow adding to their lustre. It was as though they had come from the same place.

The Queen was looking directly into Mary's clear blue eyes when she began. 'Thank you, Hector. Well done. Thank you, Mr and Mrs. Hickey. And your wonderful children. As Queen of the Faery Folk, I gratefully acknowledge your assistance to our people and graciously thank you for serving the needs of all humanity. After hundreds of years, I am so looking forward to rekindling what was once a beautiful friendship with your kind. As you well know, a few bad apples can certainly spoil the bunch, but now the time has come, the walrus said, to speak of many things, of shoes and ships and sealing wax and cabbages and... King Oberon! Finally. I thought someone would cut off my rantings long before you came,' said Queen Titiana as her anam cara appeared by her side. He, too, was dressed in his finery. All the glories of gold and green adorned his dress. Oberon's hat was reminiscent of the faeries of yore. He liked to keep older traditions alive and wasn't much up on the newer fads. Somehow, the hat remained on his head, but with his every movement it swayed from side to side. About halfway up the front was the biggest emerald Mary had ever seen.

That can't be real. It's magnificent.

'Are ye talking about me or my hat, Mary?' said the King.

Oh, not you, too.

T'isn't only Hector and me. Tis all of us and all of you. We're just havin' fun with ye. Ye'll remember soon enough, Sweet Mary.

'I think your hat is the grandest I've ever seen,' said Mary.

'Ha. Wait til ye see my flyin' hat. And now that Hector has brought us all together in Mary's Realm, we begin!'

Chapter 3:   1550 AD

The King and Queen

of Faery

His heart was still hammering when he got to the den, and he poured the whiskey with a shaky hand. He couldn't tell Titiana. If she knew how many times they'd tried to escape through the dungeon of Castle Lyonstyme, she wouldn't be preparing to leave for France. This afternoon had been a little too close for comfort, but he knew that it would be a long time before the Formorians would attempt another try.

There was no place on Earth that King Oberon loved more than his favourite home. Visitors marveled at the grandeur of the castle, set before rock faces that almost touched the clouds. Fields of heather ran up the mountains as a backdrop to the castle, sitting on rolling hills in the middle of Wales. He and Titiana loved laying on the grasses in the warm sunshine, but inside, his den was his sanctuary. And he needed a sanctuary after changing from his blood soaked riding clothes into his finery. He and his dungeon master had been thorough in disposing of the ruined clothes and cleaning up any residue of the fighting. Normally, he would share the news of the Formorian attempt to break into the Earthen realm with Titiana, but she had spent the day preparing for a long overdue holiday and he would not spoil her happiness at any cost. He had put on his forest green silk-sleeved shirt and fawn-tanned riding pantaloons, knowing that they were to sup together after the gloaming. The day was coming to an end and the fire that was roaring in the stone hearth would soon be the only light. The flames cast shadows dancing across dozens of huge oil paintings that lined the forty foot walls. Oils and sculptures created by the great masters of the last millennium unveiled scenes of Oberon's life. The paintings were portals to his memories of times long put aside.

As he waited for his Queen, he marveled at how calming the afternoon had become compared to the insanity a few hours earlier in the dungeon. Knowing she wouldn't be too much longer, he settled into his chair and gazed at his favourite painting of their wedding. Memories flooded in as he remembered how he felt as Titiana floated to shore on the wedding raft while he gazed at her with great love in his eyes. Oberon thought back to the representatives of the different realms that were standing beside him as their wedding began. World and Otherworld leaders had laid down arms and come together for a week of feasts and jocularity. Wee Folk parties were legendary, and no living being was about to let war stop them from going to the bash of the millennium. Even the Formorian contingent withdrew during times of Faery festivities, knowing that any uprising would be doomed to failure. Over the ages, Formorians had learned the hard way that Faery festivals attracted the strongest of all realms and that interruptions to their parties were very much frowned upon. Oberon smirked. Stories about Formorian sabotage attempts during ceremonies were favorites to tell, and faery folk almost wished they'd give it a try so they could crush their dark enemy once and for all.

A faery wedding was of utmost significance as faery pairings were a celebration of the gift of crossing paths. The Creator had honoured Titiana and Oberon with many gifts, but other than life itself, there was no greater gift than an anam cara, a soul partner, and opulence was the order of the day. The mysteries of the physical realm, or world of form, were often debated in the spirit realm and any chance to visit was keenly sought by beings from the Otherworlds. An invitation to a royal Faery wedding was the opportunity of a lifetime, and only the elite of mankind had ever received one. The land dwellers were so mired in forgetfulness that they had trouble recognizing the faery folk, let alone remembering attendance at a Royal Faery Wedding. Even visitors from other cultures had total amnesia after visiting, yet they enjoyed their limited time immersed in the physical experience. Oberon smiled as he remembered the invitations Titiana had conjured. On delivery day, their Lead Trooper insisted that the faeries deliver the pink bubble wrapped envelopes as his troops were needed for moat construction.

As Oberon sat in the very castle, he remembered the guests of honour marching into the Great Hall for his wedding months before the Black Death of 1347. The samurai families came in their long silken robes with intricate fans and parasols, the grand princes of Early Russia, the emperors of China, kings and queens from the temples of gold in Africa and South America. The Celts, the Greeks and the Romans joined hands with the Sumerians and the pharaohs of Egypt. The Moguls, the Asians and the Viking chiefs met the world leaders and their noble knights and entourages. It was a time of great abundance. The faery palace was filled with furniture, paintings and statues and over 1,500 good faery folk took care of every detail in the 700 rooms inside. All of the guests tried to outdo each other in the glamour and grandeur of their clothes, people and gifts. Robes made of the finest silks and in all colours were decorated with beautiful embroidery, jewels, lace and ribbons.

Although the main feasts were celebrated in the evening, the tables were replenished hourly. If the King and Queen were to walk by the tray laden tables in the course of the three week festivities, their favourite desserts, apple pies and honey cakes, would await them, fresh from the ovens. In all the courtyards, jesters made people laugh and minstrels played their instruments and sang. Near the Hall of Mirrors, Oberon and Titiana had transformed dance rooms into their gift giving halls.

In the Faery realm, wedding gifts from the married couple were displayed and restocked for all the feast days, where anyone could select gifts at any time from an assortment including adornments like beautiful brooches, arm rings and belt buckles, carved spoons and silver combs. And as opulence was the order of the day, delegations from every realm brought their own gifts for guests to share. Some of the finery included jewels from India, tea and silk from China, spices from the East Indies, sugar from Brazil and tulip bulbs from Turkey. The 21-day celebration seemed to go on forever. Day in and day out, actors, musicians and dancers entertained with music, poetry readings and skits throughout the halls and courtyards. Leisurely strolls through the palace gardens, or jousts and hunting games played out through all the days. In the evenings, there were great feasts of food and boasting.

Many of these memories had been captured in the oil paintings that held Oberon's attention. Oberon looked much the same as he had on the grand occasion of the wedding of the King and Queen of Faery. To human folk, his height belied his strength, but the Otherfolk knew the power packed into the King of the Faery and few that crossed him lived to talk about it. The fists that hurled blazing comets of fury fire were legend, but paled in comparison to the focus of intent that his being could literally manifest to change any matter in any form instantaneously. His days of havoc had long passed and Oberon chose to live a peaceful existence in the physical realm with his beloved Titiana.

Ah, it's been a wonderful life. No sooner had the thought escaped him, than Oberon's wedding celebrations were forgotten and his mind filled with the bleak human news of the day. He knew Titiana was on her way to his den to discuss strategy to help the human folk. Again. Oberon loved his home in Ireland, but equally loved his homes in Scotland and England, and did not wish to see battlegrounds on the Earthen realm if he could help it. If all failed, though, he had talked to Titiana about joining the others underground for a time. He agreed that they needed to have a holiday and consider the growing unrest across the continent. Oberon worried more about Formorians than any mankind conflict, but he was certain he had dealt their forces a considerable blow that morning.

Oberon knew that Titiana might not holiday if she suspected Formorian aggression and he had decided not to tell her about the morning attack. The growing mankind uprisings and violent times had spread to involve the Earthen royal families across the continent, and all seemed at loggerheads and were either at war or preparing for war. Titiana loved people, and wanted Oberon to rethink the underground strategy.

He remembered her words: "We're called The Shining Ones for a reason, Obie. The human folk need us. We are the Tuatha Dé Danann. We are The Children of the Goddess Danu. Remember the times when our tall and majestic forbearers decided to become "The Little People"? None on the physical realm recall what we represent. Obie, you lead the Tuatha Dé Danann and all forces of light on this side. Since time out of mind, we have fought the dark force of the Formorians. The Battle of Moytura had no happy ending. Our people lost and they were driven underground into the Sihre. There they are regrouping and strengthening the Faery Realm in a peaceful world of love. But how long must ours hide underground? Your people need you to seek the fair land. We all need you to be the leader."

Everyone is awaiting the return of beauty in the world of form. Oberon's love for Titiana over rode all relationships in his existence and she was in an uproar and wanted Oberon to do something. She had tried to intervene with the help of the prophets Ursula and Michel Nostradame, but to no avail. Oberon was her final strategy.

He had been so absorbed in the wedding memories that he hadn't noticed Titiana enter. She knew that the den was Obie's oasis of peace in the world, where he sketched or painted. His relax room. She saw he had dressed in her favourite outfit and half smiled. She had worn her latest version of the pink lace gown, normally reserved for feasts with close friends. Obie had said no other Queen of Faery had ever been so divine and he had Michelangelo paint her portrait in the pink lace. He was looking upon that very portrait as she spoke:

'Obie, I must ask you to do something against your nature.'

Oberon looked up at his Queen. Her voice sent a chill through him.

'Titiana. What has shaken you so? Is there more news?' The concern in Obie's voice was great. He stood and took her hands into his, wondering if she had somehow learned of the Formorian outbreak. Her strawberry blond hair cascaded in ringlets around her cheeks and fell to her waist. He could see forever in her clear blue eyes. He had traveled to Eagle Mountain specifically to meet the northern princess all those years ago. Stories of her courage and beauty had reached him and he knew this was the partner he had been dreaming of. His visions of her were so vivid that no thoughts came when he finally saw her, only knowing. She and her handmaiden had been picking flowers from a bush when he came around a mountain pass. He had dreamed the scene a hundred times and knew what her words would be.

'King Oberon. Welcome to Eagle Mountain.' He remembered her dress. It was a pale, shimmering blue. Sparkles danced in the sunlight. Her arms had been painted with weaves of color, but it was her face that stunned Oberon. Even though he had seen her in the visions, nothing had prepared him for the way her skin glowed. Her aura was so lovely that tears came to his eyes. Overcome, he could only muster "thank you" before dismounting and collecting himself while he bowed.

The memories were rushing back. In those early times, the centuries seemed to last forever. Oberon thought how easy it was to sum up a century in a few moments afterward. Oblivious to worldly matters, Oberon and Titiana had reveled in simply finding each other. When two such figures meet their anam cara, the world knows. Their love light shone so bright as to enlighten the faery realm and even spilled over into the darkness of the Earthern ages. Leading by example, Oberon and Titiana lived life as it was meant to be lived. They understood that creation was meant for creators and that together they formed a wondrous whole that blended in with the world of love. Instead of looking at separateness, Oberon and Titiana saw everything as connected, as one. Instead of looking at what they didn't have, they were so vocal and thankful for the many gifts bestowed upon them. They understood that there was a place for the dark realm, for the great human thinkers and the prophets in their realm. The couple was surrounded by many sages and counted them among their greatest friends. Oberon's mind was in freefall when he sensed her heavy heart.

'Obie. Obie,' Titiana's voice brought him back to his den. 'We cannot stay neutral anymore. We must go forth into the world and make some decisions. This castle has been around since Caernarvon was the capital of Wales in the ancient days and I know it will be here when we return. You know the world changes are coming fast and furious. Hector's birth portends all,' said Titiana.

The king of Faery heard a crow cawing and glanced to see the large black bird settle on a turret. He took a deep breath. He felt a love that made nothing else matter. The blackness of the crow did not register to Oberon as he watched it soar by the open window. He looked back to

Titiana, and seeing the glint from the last rays of sunshine on her hair, turned his thoughts back to their first days together. In that moment, Oberon relived the gentle peacefulness of the first time she touched his soul.

'You think about the western lands too much. It's so far from everything we know. Those crazy Vikings spent four centuries trying to settle the western lands and they're a hardy bunch! What makes you think your dreams of sails going around the world and back are anything but wishful thinking?' said Oberon.

'Oh, it's been three centuries. Surely that's enough Earthen time to get it done right? I see that same ship going around and back again and talks with the red race,' said Titiana.

'Titiana, what do you mean talks? You predicted that they'd wipe the noble red race clean off the face of Mother Earth. Call a spade a spade,' said Oberon.

'Ever since we met Ohmisseh, I know there is hope. He confirmed our suspicions about other little people living in the western lands. Remember? We thought those dreams were wishful thinking, too. He is just like you, Ob: he is a powerful leader, kind and full of love. Even your personal favourite seer says that if we intervene that it would lead to great strides for humanity and for all of us, too,' said Titiana.

'Nostradamus the Human Prophet! You're always listening to him and taking his word to heart. Stop that. He

58

certainly doesn't know anything more than we do,' said Oberon.

'Well, he was right about the University at St. Andrews, wasn't he? And the Hebrides and Stonehenge and Knowth! And King of the Experts on Seers, Michael Nostradamus knows and teaches that a good prophecy is one that can be averted. I think he's trying to help us,' said Titiana.

As Titiana was ranting, Oberon glanced at his portrait. Michael Nostradamus was a little less than middle height, and robust and cheerful, just like Oberon. His brow was high, his nose straight and his grey eyes gentle, though in wrath they would flame, just like Oberon. Even though the prophet was human, they had become fast friends on first meeting. Nostradamus was a gifted seer, but Oberon was a Faery King and privy to other wisdoms from other realms.

'Stop. He's not the answer, Titiana. Remember we can go direct to the Creator. I can remember a longer list of things Michel Nostradame was wrong about. And just imagine him saying that astrology will be ridiculed someday. Says it won't be taught at St. Andrews University anymore. Surely that is preposterous,' said Oberon.

'Oh, Ob, don't get so riled up. But I was wondering if we should go to France or maybe change our plans about taking Bezzy there and go to Knowth instead?' said Titiana.

When Titiana mentioned Knowth, Ob's mouth curled up into a sly grin and his eyes squinted.

'Ah ha! Now I know what you're up to sweet Queen of the Faery Folk! You are too funny. Why didn't you just say so? As long as I live, I will never understand the fairer folk,' said Oberon.

Both the Queen and the King broke into hearty laughter and at that moment there was a great knock at their lounge door.

'Who dares knock at the door of the King and Queen?' said Oberon.

'Tis I, Bezz, with a wee something for the Grand King and Queen,' said Bezz as she opened the door.

Titiana's most trusted handmaiden entered the den with a smile that made the King and Queen forget their troubles.

'Come, Bezz, come. We are making plans to travel to Calais and Knowth,' Oberon said with a large wink. 'Tell us when we can leave.'

Bezz knew how important this night was for the King and Queen. She was Titiana's confidante and co-conspirator and wanted to ensure that the rulers had time to reflect on the future. The King made sure their lives were full of parties and fun, but the Queen needed time alone with him to cut out all distractions and make huge decisions. Bezz had started the fire and had returned to the Golden Hall with an elaborate tea tray with the Queen's favourite treats.

'Oh, Great King. You can either wait for Doomsday or you can travel at the end of me boot, right now,' said Bezz.

Elizabeth Loretta Grodstooth, whatever would I have done without you all these years? My Bezzy.

The Hall echoed with their laughter. The King thought Bezz looked particularly graceful. Normally a very practical gnome, Bezz wore daily outfits of darker shades of green that wouldn't show the ravages of kitchen life and something comfortable that would allow her to run quickly. Yet this night, Bezz had chosen to dress as the handmaiden to the Queen that she was. Her gown flowed with a long train, sprinkles of faery dust trailing behind.

Oberon knew the magical dust was courtesy of Bezz's good friend, the faery Trinity. Trinity liked to make sure Bezz dressed the part on occasion. This night, she wore a bouffant hairstyle, to tame her wild auburn curls, and he suspected she had lined her eyes and lips with translucent colours, as she shone even more brightly than usual.

'Please join us now, Bezz. We've some things to talk over,' said the Queen solemnly.

'Why so glum all of a sudden? I've known you long enough to know your every thought and right now, I only see sad,' said Bezz.

'You know the Queen has long wanted to travel to France, Bezz; and she wants it to be a gay time with me, and you, too. I'm not sad tonight, only reflective. The Queen and I have an important project for you and after our trip, you'll be on assignment for some time.'

Bezz stopped pouring the tea.

I don't like that word assignment.

'What do you mean, 'assignment'?' said Bezz.

'Bezz, it involves you travelling with a wee babe to the western lands,' said the Queen.

'To the western lands? A babe? Without you?' Bezz said.

'Aye, my friend. I know you will love it, and I am only saddened because I will miss you so much,' said Titiana.

'And I you. But why? What babe?' asked Bezz.

'One to be born on New Year's Day, Bezz. You'll be there for his birth and shortly after, on your way to the west,' said the King.

'You must be talking about Gabby and Emma's? And you'll be having your Lead Trooper and your Handmaiden offshore at the same time?' asked Bezz.

'No, no. You'll be on this assignment alone, save for choosing a wetnurse, Bezz,' said the Queen. 'We'll leave that up to you.'

'Assignment. I don't like that word,' said Bezz.

The Queen and King smiled. *Here goes Bezz ranting about words again. If she doesn't like a word, she makes up a new crazy one.*

Bezz continued: 'It's got that ass word in it. I will make an ass out of you or me. Oh, no. That's assume. What is it that I don't like about assignment? OH, it is a sign. Omen. Mother Shipton and Michel Nostradame scary stuff,' said Bezz.

'Well, yes and no, Bezz,' said the King. 'Both of the Queen's good friends have seen something happening between the western lands and us for some time. No scary stuff for you; you've been chosen because we trust you completely and know your prowess with Light to be of the finest calibre.'

'So the wee one will be in need of protection?' said Bezz.

'More than that, Bezz; he will be in need of guidance,' said the Queen.

'He?' said Bezz.

'Aye, Bezz. Ob and I have long known that the world is shifting. This newborn will help to lead the way into a new, peaceful world,' said Titiana.

'I have so many dillykind questions, but no doubt that I am the right gnome. I will do my best to fulfill this dream,' said Bezz.

'There is one thing that both seers talked about that I sense to be true,' said Oberon. 'They said that we are all in for a wild ride in 1555 and to hold on to our seats. In the grand tradition of the Faery Folk, I think it best that we party for a few months beforehand. You ladies make the plans and make them fast. Wherever we're going, I want us to be gone before the week ends. After your tea, please join me in my chambers, Oh Queen of Mine. I'm sure your Bezz will have a few questions for you now. Until then, toodles.'

And with that, the King departed behind the golden drapes near the firewall, taking the back stairs up to his chambers. The Queen turned to Bezz and held out her arms.

'Come here, Bezz and sit with me. I've been trying to muster the courage to tell you all of this and it had to be tonight. I'm glad of it, so we can make plans. I don't know if we'll ever see each other after you ship out and that is why I don't like to think about it,' said Titiana.

'Now, now, Queenie. We've had a good go at it and have shared so many special times. We'll have more, I know it,' said Bezz.

'Did you say Knowth!?' said Titiana.

Both ladies laughed loud and long. They had fond memories from Knowth. The ladies talked for a long spell. Memories of the Celtic priests from Tara, the Druids, and their mischievous actions made them laugh. One Druid was purported to have embedded the roar of a lion into the large stone at the gates of Tara. He said the rock would roar for all to hear on the Isle of Destiny when the True King returned to the Seat of Destiny. Since the time of the Tuatha Dé Danann, the Faery people had experienced many world views held by the people of Earth.

At any given time, there were several conflicting world views and many conflicts, usually over land. The Romans had been horrified by human sacrifice and feared the Celtic tradition of skulls on gateways and poles. *Memento mori.* For a few centuries, the ancient Greeks and Romans battered the local Celts. These adversaries embodied two ideas of the world in dark times. There was that Greco-Roman rationalism with all their logic and engineering prowess and then there were the Celts and their magic and intuition. The gruesome bloodshed between the Romans and the Celts did not end until the Faery Folk intervened.

'Surely as sure can be, we'll gladly take the credit for all the good in the world! But isn't it wild how things went so wrong after Jeremiah The Prophet and Tea Telphi of Egypt arrived in Tara? With her wedding to an Irish King, the Tuatha Dé Danann thought that all the world views were meshing, but somehow people allow the greedy fearmongers to rule the roost and keep falling back to square one,' said Bezz.

'Ha. I know you're right, Bezz, but one of these times the world will return to love forever and ever amen! Looking back, the conquerors conquer for a time and then along come some new plunderers. Remember when the Danes started invading the eastern shores of England? Must have been in the early 800s, but it wasn't until that Canute came along that the ball started rolling. Wasn't he the King of England in the early 1000s? And the Norman invasions were soon after that. But I don't think anything holds a candle to the 500-year rule of Romans in England! And they're long gone now.'

'Aye, they all sought the fair land and won it, for awhile. When will the human race learn that we are all of Mother Earth? Will the golden days ever come again? I heard the Earthen Folk sing this new song about the new land:

Let's away to the new land where plenty sits queen
O'er as happy as country as ever was seen:
She blesses her subjects, both little and great,
With each good house, and a pretty estate.
There's wood, and there's water, there's wild fowl and tame;
In the forest good ven'son, good fish in the stream,
Good grass for our cattle, good land for our plough,
Good wheat to be reap'd, and good barley to mow.
No landlords are there the poor tenants to tease,
No lawyers to bully, nor stewards to seize;
But each honest fellow's a landlord and dares
To spend on himself the whole fruit of his cares.
They've no duties on candles, no taxes on malt,

Nor do they, as we do, pay sauce for their salt;
But all is as free as in those times of old
When poets assure us the age was of gold.'

'Oh, Bezz, that's just what Ob and I are talking about. Taking care of everyone, not just the few. But let's talk about fun stuff. It's time to enjoy each other. Maybe we'll be able to get you back for a visit. Oh, I'm probably fooling myself because I'm so worried I'll never see you again. Oh, I'm getting sad again. This Isle of Destiny shall certainly miss her Bezz,' the Queen said.

'Someday, Titiana. We'll be off on some adventures and then we'll get back together, ok? Someday, someway. So, no more looking glum, chum. I'll sing and harp now to cheer you and then send you off happy to our King,' said Bezz.

She started humming as she danced across the Hall to where the harp sat. Bezz's voice lulled the Queen to happier times and she ended the night making a new song:

My Queen sends mists of happy, floating 'cross the sky;
Her wee folk all run out to play, for they don't like to cry...
They see her flying high above
And send her hearts full of love,

'Tis our Queen we see so fair
Up above us, of the air
Queen, Queen Titiana
Oh where is your King
She called, "I'm flying off to see him now,
In our land of dreams"
And you, my wee folk, go
And enjoy your land of dreams
Enjoy your land of dreams.

'Ah Sweet Bezz. I'll go now, happily,' said Titiana as she disappeared behind the golden drapes.

Chapter 4: 1550 AD

Arrival at the Land of

Friendship

Bezzy had had enough. She'd be talking to the Queen about this assignment. They'd gone off course. *No fault of the Cap'n mind you. Those waves looked like walls. And so many of them. By the time that utha storm had passed, we were closer to wamdam Viking ground than New Found Lande. Those damnation Vikings were surrounding us, too. I could just feel them. Great Gratitude thoughts to Goddess for the blanket of protection. I could feel those swirls, too. Forty-eight days at sea had taken a toll on wee Hector. That child was a strapping one when they set out on the one side of the Atlantic and a soliderferous one on t'other, but not quite as robust. Give him a few days. Nostradamus said there'd be some delays, but predicted an uneventful and successful crossing. I guess the old seer doesn't think walls as high as castles are too eventful. He mentioned about the stars and right timing. Why didn't we set sail a few weeks* later for goodnessgraciousness?

After centuries of working with or on mankind, the Queen's heart was warmed to learn of tribes living in the western lands from Nostradamus. Bezzy thought back to when she first heard of them. *I'll never forget his words. Heard them firsthand, firstime from the man himself: 'There is a land across the pond, a land of treasures ancient and new and there dwell a peoples with a worldview such as you.'*

When Nostradamus had predicted the formation of an alliance, the Queen had been adamant about taking the first step. In her own way, she made contact with the leader of a faraway tribe and sent the message that an Ambassador was coming forthwith. Nostradamus's ending words were ringing in Bezz's ears: '*Floating on the wind road, under the North Star's guiding light, your people will cross the global seas, fighting off disease, and create a pact anew to renew an old pact.' That seer sure did vex a soul sometimes. The Queen couldn't even figure that one out. Or so she said.*

Solid ground. The image of Hector's wetnurse running, almost flying, down the plank and onto the beach made Bezzy smile. *Myrgth is a goodgoodie girl and Hector loves her. She's doing her job and the ship's captain got us here in one piece. Not even one lost life and that in itself is strange these days. Twas a good crew. Now the work beginneth.* The ship landed, as ordered by the King and Queen, and baby Hector was designated as the Ambassador of The Little People.

The shoreline was a sight for sore eyes. Beaches and evergreens as far as the eyes could see. Rock faces cut from the glaciers that had carved the continent thousands of years before. Water thick and dancing with fish. An Emerald Isle of Old. All of Mother Earth's creations were breathtaking, but it was the abodes on shore that captured Bezz's attention. They certainly didn't look the same as back home. Many single dwellings were interspersed among several larger versions. The basic conical structure seemed to be five poles of wood lashed together with some kind of rope at the top and spread out at the bottom. She noticed hoops tied under the poles, just down from the top, acting as a brace. There were shorter poles tied to the hoop all around to support the covering. Bezz had never seen anything like it. The covering seemed to be sheets of bark from some of the trees surrounding the encampment, though no trees seemed to be stripped. These white bark sheets were laid over the poles like shingles, starting from the bottom and overlapping as they worked up the dwelling. Extra poles were laid over the outside to hold the bark down. She noticed the swirls of smoke arising from most of the openings at the tops. The larger versions were quite a bit longer and had two fireplaces, or two swirlings of smoke rising. Bezz thought these must be smoke houses for cooking and wondered where the tall, dark human beings built their castles.

Lost in thought, Bezz was looking for a welcoming party as the ship docked near a jutting rock platform. There were hundreds of people crowding around the rock. Spring was in the air, yet the men's garments included robes of fur. She noticed the feet were bound with furs or skins, too. Bezz wondered if these were ceremonial or everyday wear. Both men and women had leggings of skin or hides and loincloths decorated with many colours. Women wore similar robes to men, wrapped around their bodies under their arms like a bath towel with thongs over the shoulders acting like suspenders. A handsome people. Bezz noticed commotion around one of the larger structures and saw her first glimpse of the leader.

Whewser. He's a handsome one. Must be seven feet tall and that thick, plaited hair half way down his... BEZZY!

Acting as the official Ambassador, Bezzy was joined by Hector and Myrgth. While the Captain and crew were led to a longhouse for washing up and eating, Bezz and hers were led by a dancing entourage to the handsome one. Bezz was happy she had chosen Myrgth to join the expedition. She had a lovely nature and calmed Hector, who was sleeping peacefully in her arms. As they entered the largest of the Mi'kmaq structures, Bezz's eyes adjusted to the darkness and the midday fireglow. She smiled.

Their guide stood aside and said, 'Grand Chief Kaqtukwow,' as a sign of greeting.

'Tis truly an honour, Chief. I am Elizabeth Loretta Grodstooth, Acting Ambassador of King Oberon and Queen Titiana of the Little People Nation of Alandthatis,' Bezz said as she handed the scroll to the Grand Chief and continued speaking. 'I shall represent my King and Queen and the Little People until Young Ambassador Hector reaches the age of 11, at which time you will know him as Ambassador Hector. As you know, the Queen respectfully requested that Hector be raised as and by your people with my guidance, so that our two nations may join as one. Hector's wetnurse here is Myrgth. The King and Queen look forward to your representative's imminent arrival on the other side as well,' said Bezz.

While Bezz spoke, she was remembering some of the fascinating history of the Mi'kmaq people as she had heard from the Queen herself:

The ancient ones came to their land, the land called Terra Nova or New Founde Land, thousands of years before the rise of the great civilizations of Mesopotamia and Egypt. Their ancestors returned there after the Great Ice Age or Jenu at least 11,000 years ago, following the caribou across the tundra. By 5,000 BC, the people began calling themselves Nikmaq, or 'my

73

kin friends' in honour of their awareness of the spiritual and collective unity of existence.

Even though they looked more like Celts on the outside, Bezzy intuitively knew that the Mik'maki people came from the same place as the Little People, wherever that may have been.

'And Chief, please call me Bezzy or Bezz. It will make me feel at home. I have some gifts for you from our King and Queen and some stories to share. Please tell me how to honour you first: stories or gifts?'

'Bezz, my Mi'kmaq name is Kaqtukwow. A thousand welcomes. A hundred thousand welcomes be before you, Myrgth and boy Hector. Our community is full of gratitude for your safe arrival. We are honoured by your arrival and look forward to an alliance brought about by the Creator. Through our visions, I have been sharing our stories with your Queen and now know some of yours, too. I look forward to hearing many more of yours. We shall share stories everyday after eating together. When the day comes, we eat and share dreams. When the night comes, we eat and share stories.

'Our land is a place where the life-forces or manitu of stones, rivers, coast, oceans, animals and people reside in harmony, where our Mi'kmaq nation honours all of these life-forces, manitu'k. Our worldview includes order and sharing between all things, animals and peoples in this realm. Only the unborn children in the invisible sacred realm have any ultimate knowing of the oneness, as is truth with your people,' Chief

74

Kaqtukwow spoke slowly and Bezzy saw clearly why she was sent to this new land. He continued: 'We have grown like the grasses and trees you see around you, Bezz. For thousands of years we have lived in harmony with the land and our neighbours and now you have come to us when our way of life is threatened. I have shown your Queen that our people are dying. I have shared with your Queen my visions. She among them.'

Bezz was so taken with Kaqtukwow's words and voice that she didn't notice the young warrior move to her side. His presence startled her and she jumped.

'I apologize, son. I did not hear ye approach,' Bezz said as she touched the shaken lad.

'He brings you dunk,' said Chief Kaqtukwow. 'His name is Lkimu, meaning 'he sends' in your words. Lkimu has been chosen to shadow you.'

'Shadow me?' said the astonished Bezz.

'Yes. Niskam, our Creator, has come to me in a vision. You are the protector of The One Who Must Be Protected. Lkimu is stellar in his accomplishments and is honoured to guard you. This must be so.'

'I accept your help, Lkimu, and am full of gratitudededelight at your kindess and humbled by your vision, Chief,' said a smiling Bezz.

Wow. What a strange land. I LOVE IT! Lkimu was nearly as tall as the Chief and had the same kindness glowing from within. Bezz accepted the brightly painted earthen mug and drank deeply. She was taken by the warm sweetness of the drink and felt tingly when done.

'Dunk is dedelightfullydedelicious. M'mm. Thanks so much, my new friend,' said Bezz.

As they had been standing throughout the initial introductions, Lkimu showed the guests where to sit as the Chief sat down. 'You are very welcome, my new friend, and please sit in our circle of friends,' said the smiling Lkimu.

Lkimu's hand swept in a grand gesture of welcoming and Bezz noticed, for the first time, that the floor was lined with fir twigs, woven mats and animal furs. There was a large hide that acted as a door covering and Bezz had no idea where most of the hides and furs came from. She had a lot to learn about this new land. She wondered where their real dwellings were but said, 'Myrgth told the Captain about 'the land of friendship' on the way over here. Myrgth, please share with everyone your story.'

Myrgth's face visibly reddened. She was quiet around some folks, but had always been a chatty companion to Bezz.

'Of course, Mrs. Grodstooth,' Myrgth quietly said. 'There's no use standing up to Mrs. Grodstooth; she always wins!' Feeling comfortable, Myrgth looked from the Grand Chief to Lkimu and started her story. 'While we were in the middle of a huge storm on the ocean, the ship was being thrown around like a toy. In the midst of these waves as big as castles, the Captain took us into the middle of the bottom of the ship and started yelling stories or poems or singing over the thunderous crashing sounds. Wee Hector never skipped a beat. He's a man-child and a brave one at that.'

'Stop it Myrgth,' Bezz interrupted and smiled at her. Looking to the chief and his aide, Bezz continued: 'She tends to talk on an on to distraction. Reminiscent of myself! Now tell the gentlemen the real story.'

'Oh, thank you, Mrs. Grodstooth. I do tend to digress. Well, a friend of mine hails from the Emerald Isle on the eastern coast, Molly. She came to our house last summer for a visit with her family and told us a tale of a confederacy of kinfolk from this side of the pond. I told Mrs. Grodstooth that these wee folk claim to have been stranded here over a thousand years ago and long forgotten by the likes of Queen Titiana. Molly said they gave up trying to contact the King and Queen in the world of form and started to send dream visions instead. Molly said that you call your land The Land of Friendship.

The Chief smiled. He had not told the Queen this name, but the child was right.

'I know these little peoples. They are a part of our Wabanaki Confederacy and their representative travels to our village as we speak. When I made first contact with your Queen, I thought she was also from our Land of Friendship.'

Hector let out a shrill cry. The small group laughed as the Chief welcomed him: 'A thousand welcomes, wee Hector. A hundred thousand welcomes young Ambassador.'

'Now that we are all in a circle, let us announce every person and their intentions with our red willow bark ceremony,' commanded the Chief. 'As is our custom, our new friends, we shall smoke tobacco from red willow bark, bearberry leaves and wild tobacco from The Creator's land. Apiknajit is long gone and our new crops are bountiful,' said Kaqtukwow as Lkimu looked up at him. 'Ah, yes, Lkimu reminds me that I must teach you about our colourful words. Apiknajit is our word for your month of February. Your words say 'snow-blinder'. You have come at my favourite time of the year. Everything is new again. Life is all around, even in the midst of the coming sickness. Your arrival time bodes well for the future of our land and our friendship. Let us rejoice.'

With these words, the Chief stood up and several women entered the tent to stand at his side. The women were tall, some with their hair falling loose around their face and some with their hair plaited like the men. All were kindly looking on the nursing babe in Myrgth's arms.

'My soul friend, Naki, mother of our children, meet our new friends.' To greet the honoured guests, Naki offered Bezz a round box made out of the same bark as their smoke house. The top and sides were designed with brightly coloured geometric mosaics.

'She is the daughter of our Shaman; like your doctor, only better,' smiled the Chief.

Naki laughed, 'Kaq is funny and makes everyone smile. All of us are so happy you have arrived safely and your Captain tells us there are no illnesses. We shall celebrate with thanks properly as soon as you have been comforted with food and drink. I have ensured that your crew is taken care of and now I would love to meet the new Ambassador.'

'Myrgth, the child will want to meet our new Queen now,' said Bezz. 'Queen Naki, this box is magnificent. Thanks so much for your kindness. I, too, have something for you from Queen Titiana herself. She told me to tell you in no uncertain terms: from a queen to a queen. We shall present it to you after we sup.

As Myrgth held the baby upward, Hector reached his arms out for Naki's embrace.

'Look, girls, he's too adorable,' Naki hugged him and then showed him to her three daughters. 'My girls have offered to shadow the Ambassador,' smiled Naki as her daughters surrounded the baby.

Naki took a soft, tan skin from her belt and swaddled Hector in it. 'You will find that after death our animals provide warmth and comfort for us. I am gifting The Ambassador with our finest swaddling cloth,' said Naki.

Bezz reached over to touch it and was amazed at its softness.

'It's as soft as a weebabybottom, Naki. Hector will love it, thank you,' said Bezz.

79

'Inside your box is some sweetgrass for you, Bezz. Have you heard of sweetgrass?'

'No, I haven't,' said Bezz as she opened the box. Inside she saw braids of milky green grasses, circling around. 'What's it for? And please tell me about the box. What is it made of? And those magnificocacreation colours? Where do they come from?'

'So many questions. All of us have questions. We will sit in our circle and show her the sweetgrass ceremony, Naki. Let us begin while you tell her about the making of the birchbark box.'

'Our dwellings are called 'wikuom', or wigwam, and we make them from the bark of our birch trees. When we move, we take our birchbark tree homes with us. They are waterproof and easy to carry. You saw our canoes, too, Bezz? They are made of the same bark, as is the wigwam as is your new box. I have personally made this box as a gift for you. The needles or quills you see are from an animal called a porcupine and I have dyed the quills in these bright colours. We use the colours from roots, bark, leaves and flowers as dye. I will show you someday soon and we will create together. Meanwhile, I have filled your box with sweetgrass, as I want to ensure that you always have what you need here in The Land of Friendship,' said Naki.

As she expressed her thanks to Naki, Bezz wondered if she'd died and gone to Heaven. She looked around the wigwam and smiled at her good fortune.

Chapter 5: 1550 AD

The Vision of the

Three Crosses

After the long journey at sea, the three newcomers settled into the comfort of their own home in the Land of Friendship. Their wigwam felt roomy compared to the hovels in the old country, and the girls were happy to have the space to keep little Hector happy. Bezz was used to dampness and a chill in the air in the castles and appreciated the warmth of the space, especially after the cramped and dank ship. With the baby sleeping soundly, Bezz and Myrgth had time to share their thoughts about the marvels of the new country and were happy to settle in for the evening.

'Bezz, I loved that sweetgrass ceremony. I think wee Hector approved, too,' said Myrgth.

'Wheezer. Such copious amounts of smoke. And the smell. You haven't lived on Goddess Green Earth until you've smelled her burning. Twas as lovely as anything I've ever experienced Myrgth. And Naki's Dad… what was his name, eh?'

'Shadeenok'

'Aye. When Shadeenok danced around me with those feathers, I couldn't stop smiling if I'd tried. Did you see that shell? What kind of shell was that? Must of been a moon shell because I'm sure there's nothing like it on Earth!'

'I don't know. But that smoke! Did you hear Naki? She said you must have some kind of energy because the smoke wouldn't stop. There was a lot more around you than me, Mrs. Grodstooth.'

'Rubbland and rubberrubbish, Myrgth! You've more energy than Hector and me put together. But what about when that feather sounded off? It went snap, snap, snap all around. What with Shadeenok's voice wailing and the feather snapping, it was all too grand.'

'Did you hear Naki? When Shadeenok was putting more sweet grass in the shell, she came over to ready me for my turn. She whispered…'

Myrgth was cut off in mid sentence when the heavy hide door was swept aside and suddenly Lkimu stood in full grandeur in their wigwam.

'Kimono! I mean Lkimu! I've never seen a shadow make a more shadelivingshady entrance,' blurted Bezzy.

82

'My apologies, friends. But the Chief has sent me with an urgent message: you must come at once,' said Lkimu.

'Can you tell us what it's about at least, Lkimu? How's a lady to get any beauty sleep in a wigwam anyway?' asked Bezzy.

'It is a custom for all leaders of tribes to gather in the Chieftan's wigwam upon the arrival of any new leader. For proper greetings,' said Lkimu.

'Well, we just got on our new skivvies, for goodness gracious Goddess sakes. Now, we'll get them off again, we will. And you can't tell me that you go behooding and barging into Naki's wigwam like this? Even in the hovels at Knowth we have a door system. What about here, Lkimu?' said Bezzy.

'You're funny, Bezzy. You make happy. This is good. I will teach you about our door system tomorrow. Much to learn. I await you and I accompany you now,' said Lkimu.

Bezz didn't miss the look that exchanged between Myrgth and Lkimu. *Ah ha. She's met her match. She's so tiny, but a veritable explosion of light inside. Could see it in her eyes.*

'Lkimu, is it the western little people?' said Myrgth.

'The scouts say they are seven strong,' said Lkimu as he pulled aside the door hide and disappeared as quickly and as silently as he'd entered.

'Never a duller moment, eh, Myrgth. Seven strong. The Queen would be pleased. Any diplomatic delegation must be of seven, unless...' Bezz's voice trailed off.

'Unless what?' said Myrgth.

'Never you mind, young lady. And I saw you looking at Lkimu. And he at you. Hurry now. No tardying a delegation of seven or the King of the Land of Friendship for that matter!' said Bezzy.

'Mrs. Grodstooth, will we ever figure out these new customs and clothes? I love the undergarment. Lkimu's sister said it was made of fox fur or hide or something. It's divine and fine. Oh, how do you say that? It's divinely finely. That's it. Divinely finely, isn't it?' said Myrgth.

'If you're to be living with me, day in and day out, Miss Myrgth Isabella Caste, you'd best be learning how to speak proper Bezzfull. Not to mention Mi'kmaq while you're at it,' said Bezzy as she fitted her robe about her and adjusted its belt. Myrgth looked stunning when she put on her new land of friendship robe. She and Bezzy were much shorter in stature than the Mi'kmaq, but their inner light shone clearly through their outer beauty. Myrgth's hair hung long past her waist, a thick and luscious strawberry blonde, and her eyes twinkled when she smiled. She had always laughed a lot and even the journey hadn't dampened her spirits. Bezz thought that Myrgth's mere presence on the ship had played a huge role in boosting morale and a major reason for no loss of life. Bezz noticed Myrgth eying the sleeping baby and was touched by the look of love.

'Wee Hector. An angel divine, that one. Finely divinely, he is. Let us, nay, let you, swaddle the young lad and be on our way,' said Bezz.

'Yes, Ma'am. We don't want to keep anyone waiting on our account. I'm ready, willing and able. Did you see Lkimu's arm painting?' said Myrgth.

'Did, too. Saw it right away this afternoon. I'd say it has something to do with why we're here, but you ask him. I wondered about the significance of the three crosses. There, ready?' said Bezzy as she pulled at the hide to exit the wigwam.

'Speak of the devil! We were just talking about that,' said Bezz as she touched the young man's arm. Lkimu smiled and turned to guide his new friends through the maze of people and wigwams. As they walked along, Bezz noticed the curious stares of the people and smiled to everyone. Now that the gloaming had passed, there were fewer children, but a fair number of adults were chatting while straightening up the home area. Bezz was happy when she heard one of the people call the acreage around the firepit the 'home area'; the

Mi'kmaq had a true sense of community. There were four large two fire wigwams centred around the pit, at least 200 yards back, creating this community space. Then, circling out around were many wigwams, large and small, in every direction. Kaq had gifted one of the larger wigwams to Bezz, Hector and Myrgth. Bezz had been so pleased when she learned the wigwams were their permanent homes, not just smoke houses. These peoples really were in touch with Mother Earth and all of her glories.

Bezz wondered if Shadeenok the Shaman would be pulling out the sweetgrass again. The ceremony comforted her, almost as much as being on solid ground again. As they walked into the Chief's wigwam, her question was answered. Bezz saw old Shadeenok open up his fur belt and begin to prepare for the ceremony. She smiled as she saw him placing sweet grass into the shell.

Kaq began as the guests and Mi'kmaq settled into their assigned seats:
'A thousand welcomes to Mikmaki, The Land of Friendship, Our Creator, Niskam, has surrounded us with his great waters and Nikmaq, our allies. The water travelers call our home the place of many people. We have lived for thousands of years through the bounty of our Creator. The waters that gave us life have sustained us. Now the waters have brought a new challenge. Tonight I gather you to prepare for a ceremony

and a tabagie which beings when the sun is centered after the sunrise. Yes, we will feast and all leaders from the Wabanaki Confederacy will be here. I am sharing my story with The Little People tonight, to begin the ceremony energy.

When our ancestor Kluskap discovered the land across the ocean, now called Europe, he came home to warn us about the coming of the blue eyes. Then the ancient spirits told him that the people would come floating on the wind. We have met these new neighbours. We are learning from their ways. They like the furs, the meat, and the fish. We have much to offer their peoples. They have much knowledge to offer us.

I am full of gratitude that you have all arrived safely, as we have much work to do in a short time. I have called for this Council to share a vision of our ancestor whose name I was gifted. Kaqtukwow The Old has come to me to share from The Land That Has No Time. I call this message The Vision of The Three Crosses.

After Kluskap, came the vision of our ancestor Intuknokeet. She told of a small island floating toward Mikmaqi. We know the meaning of the visions and have welcomed the tall ships that bring the blue eyes. The new prophecy is an old prophecy returned through me. By tradition, we begin all stories by speaking the word N'karnayoo, 'Of the Old Time'. Every tale relates back to the ancient days, to see where we have come from and then to look to where we are going. The prophecy is a vision told by beings in the Old Time, at the beginning of the Ice Age, Jenu.

I saw a young man carrying three crosses. He brought them to me and offered them as a gift. He said that there was a purpose for each cross and that my people would survive if each purpose was discovered and used properly. He said the first cross would serve the people in times of conflict with nature and other peoples. The second cross would grant safe passage on long voyages and with new experiences. The last cross was to serve the Councils, to aid them in making proper decisions for future generations. I drew these symbols from the vision and shared with all other families.' He gestured to the paintings adorning the birch bark all around the wigwam.

'As the vision continued, Kaqtukwow The Old showed me our village from his time. There were hard times, famine. With the coming of the vision, he gathered his people and they knew that if they united with other tribes they would survive. Awitkatultik, meaning 'many families living under one house', was organized. There were six sakamowit. The hard times ended but the legacy of the three crosses remained. Then, the starving St. Lawrence Iroquoians of the Haudenosaunee, the Six Nations of Iroquois, attacked. Their advances were ended through talks and they joined the three crosses tribes. Peace and prosperity returned to the united peoples. Kaqtukwow The Old explained an ancient symbol of

*the petroglyphs, which may still be seen carved in the rocks
throughout our lands. There is a ring of seven hills and seven
crosses. In the middle are symbols of the sun and the moon,
which together represent the Creator.*

*And though we call our nation Awitkatultik, the name
meaning many families living under one house, we came to
be known as the allied peoples, or Mi'kmaq. Now, we hear
news about terrible diseases from our wikamow, these
extended families. Their sayas, leaders, will arrive soon. We
have a common language, culture and spirituality and all
know the legacy of the three crosses. The first cross was to
allow us to unite and prosper. The second cross we are
holding high now, my friends. It is with this cross that we
have met our blue-eyed friends and welcomed them as our
own. When they come to our shores, these sea-worn
adventurers, they are weakened from illness and craving
fresh water, meat and green vegetables. The Mi'kmaq greet
all strangers with their universal concept of Nikmaq, friends.
This second cross, the cross to offer safe passage for
voyageurs and for new experiences, is our challenge. Our
Shaman has told me that we are entering the sixth world and
facing an annihilation of our people. He says that many
Mi'kmaq must pass on ahead. They are to be in The Land
That Has No Time. The people that are left behind must carry
the second cross for all of us.*

Bezzy, since our first meetings, I have learned from your Queen that you come from Alandthatis; our Little People of the Wabanaki Confederacy know you as The Little People from The Seas. For some reason known only to the Creator, your Queen has not known about the Little People of the Kawarthas. The Confederacy hoped that by receiving an Ambassador from your people, a new conduit of communication would open up to help us through this devastation. You must know this history, as the prophecy includes you. It has been revealed that an Ambassador Hector will carry the third cross, representing Mi'kmaq, when the time of the seventh world unfolds. At that time, Mi'kmaq will encompass all human allies.'

Bezzy listened with rapt attention, not moving or making a sound. She had so many questions, but waited for Kaq to finish. *Visions. Annihilation. Seventh World. Hector will carry the third cross. It all sounds so ominous.*

Kaq stood.

'Now, we dunk. We must keep our energy strong for all that is to come. But now, I need you to be awake and alert for the arrival of our allies. You have questions and they will be answered. I have more to share. Much more. Our time grows short,' said Kaq.

'Wheezer. What kind of annihilation? Are you saying that the Wee Folk might help to prevent this? Or it cannot be avoided? What kind of diseases?' said Bezzy as she gently touched Kaq's arm. She searched his eyes for answers and saw only profound sadness.

'Bezz, let us dunk. All will be revealed with time,' Kaq said.

'Well, then, Mr. Chief Kaq, for that load of evasiveness, you get a big hug. Did you know that we have a saying, the Wee Folk of the Seas? It's 'G'ae a Hug, Get a Hug'. G'ae means give with an accent, folks. So everybody has to hug the closest person to them, right now, before we dunk!' said Bezz, effectively clearing the heaviness in the air. Everyone laughed and enjoyed the moment, the hilarity of the tall humans and the Wee Folk hugging felt by all.

Naki's girls came in carrying woven baskets filled with treats for the late night guests. The Mi'kmaq had lifetimes of helping out starved sailors and knew just what to feed them in terms of drink and sustenance and when. Their shrunken bellies needed time to get used to the land of plenty.

'We are giant L'nuk to your Wee L'nuk,' said Lkimu to Myrgth.

'L'nuk? Is that feet?' said Myrgth.

'Ha. No, Myrgth. It is how we call ourselves since time remembers. L'nuk simply means 'the people'. Once visitors came, they saw we had a large confederacy of friends and began calling nikmaq and then Mikmaq, meaning friends,' said Lkimu.

'That's lovely, Lkimu. But you don't have to think of me as 'wee'. I'm wee in height only. I have a giant light within,' said Myrgth.

'I see that light shining from your eyes, Myrgth,' said Lkimu.

'Lkimu. Oh. Um. I see the picture on your wigwam and the one on your arm is a little bit different. Why is the middle cross so much bigger on your arm?' said Myrgth, changing the topic. When she reached over and touched his arm painting, she felt a jolt of electricity run through her. Lkimu, too, felt the charge.

'Ah. You are so full of energy. It has come into mine,' said Lkimu.

'Tarnation eagle talons. What has come unto you, Lkimu?' interjected Bezz.

'Oh, Bezzy. We were just talking about Lkimu's arm painting.'

'And by all the saints and St. Patrick, I'm sure of it,' said Bezz.

'You are funny. As you heard in the Chief's story, our people live under the three crosses. When a boy becomes a warrior, he earns the right to wear the three crosses,' said Lkimu.

'A boy? What about girls?' asked Myrgth.

'They too are so honoured. Many girls choose the three crosses and many choose the Creator symbol. It depends on the time of year and the ceremony for some. The children often wear 'heaven' to remind them that we are a part of heaven on earth,' said Lkimu.

'And what…' said Bezz before being interrupted by Kaq's booming voice.

'Please join the circle again, friends,' said Kaq. Bezz had noticed that the Chief had been taken aside by one of the older men, who seemed to be updating him on the outside world. Time seemed to lose way to ceremony when in a wigwam. Bezz had heard that story telling was an art form with these peoples and that some stories would last for days. She smiled inside when she resumed her seat.

'Forgive the shortness of the break, but, as I said, we have much ground to cover. I am told that the travellers will arrive within the hour,' said Kaq.

'Bezz, you have asked some poignant questions. I cannot answer all of them as only Our Creator knows for certain,' said Kaq.

'Chief, you tell me how the Wee Folk of the Seas can help and you have my word as the Acting Ambassador that our help shall be yours for the asking,' said Bezz.

'I know not what I ask, in terms of toil on your people, but I know what I must ask,' said Kaq. 'The blue eyes have brought disease to our shores. With the second cross held high, we face what our ancestors prophesied. The few who remain must keep our stories alive and live with our worldview strong in the midst of the coming chaos. The day will come when Ambassador Hector will carry the third cross so that all people may know the way of the L'nuk. As above, so below.'

'Must we accept this fate? I shall not go quietly, Kaq, nor do I want your people to...' said Bezz.

'Bezz, Bezz. It has been ordained. We see only one part of the picture. Shadeenok says we must know sorrow to fully experience joy. Tell us in your words, Shadeenok, of why our peoples must go through this fire,' said Kaq.

The old shaman smiled. He said, 'Let me share this with you.' With those words, Shadeenok entered the middle of the circle and unrolled his belt, pulling out his special possessions as he spoke. 'I sat at my grandmother's knee and heard the same stories that you heard at your grandmother's knee. And before us, she sat at her grandmother's knee and so on, back until the magical time and place in which there were no boundaries between human, animals and the divine. Humans were at peace with the animals and spoke their language. There was a mingling between the divine and human. Wild and tame had no meaning. Animals and humans could speak together, sometimes humans learning animal speak and sometimes the animals learned the human way. With these stories, we are aware of our awareness. Our awareness of all that is. An awareness that we live at one with and in harmony with all that is. We do not possess or own anything but our existence. We are a part of it all; we are L'nuk. The Creator has given us the most precious gift of all, life. With life comes the responsibility to share. L'nuk share with the stones, trees, rivers, oceans, animals and with all peoples. My son, Kaq. You call this a fire through which we must pass. A fire suggests total purification. The Creator has shared this land for thousands of years, a peaceful time, with our peoples and we choose now to come home for a time of rest. We shall walk through the fire, home. Our brothers, that we have welcomed as our own, will have their time here. They, too, will learn to share. Some of us will stay as guides. When we return in numbers, there will be no illness or disease. All that and even death will be of the past and soon forgotten. All that is, will be. Now, we will celebrate and prepare for those who will be left behind,' said Shaman Shadeenok.

'Thank you, Father. Your words inspire me. Spirit is here with us,' said Kaq as Naki swept the door aside to announce the arrival of the Delegation of Seven.

Chapter 6: 1550 AD

The Trip to

Misty-Eyed Falls

It had been one week since their arrival and Bezz was just getting into the routine of the village. *Well, it was more a town or a city. Didn't look like many folks at first glance, but there must be tens of thousands easily.* She wondered where they all slept at night. *I've slept like a baby since we got here. Don't know if it's the lovely freshoffitis air or the comfytible pelts on the grasses.*

'Bezz, we're going to the falls after breakfast; are you up for it?' asked Lkimu as he joined the walking Bezz.

'Yes, ohnellykins, yes! If there is anywhere on GodGoddesses Green Earth that I would like to spend my time, it is at those Misty Eyed Falls. Are you going to eat now? Who is all going?' said Bezz as they walked toward Kaq's wikoum.

'Yes, I'll join you. We'll see, but I think the Chief has asked the wee folk, too. He wants to do a sweet grass ceremony near the falls and thank Creator for our good fortune. He's quite a leader. In all of our despair, Chief tells us to think about what we do have, not about what we don't have. And especially to give thanks by enjoying everything good in our lives right now.'

'I know. I love the way he talks. I still can't wrap my hugglehead around the fact that so many people are dying right around us. It saddens me to the beyond, to the deepest deeps of my soul,' said Bezz.

'The warrior in me knows this is the ultimate spiritual battle; but the little boy in me cries, Bezz. I know the Chief says we will shine in your Tir-na-nOg soon, and it sounds so incredible, but I love the bliss and blessings on Mother Earth and I think I'll miss them when we're gone,' said Lkimu.

'Please, please. Let's not think about it, Lkimu. It tears at me very heart. I know Myrgth is casting spells to the north, east, west and south of all Creation,' said Bezz, smiling sadly. 'She is trying to change the direction of the wind so no ill will befall the village. After just meeting you, she doesn't want to lose you so soon. She loves the peaceful way of life here.'

'Since the healers have arrived in full force, I was wondering if the Chief would have new visions,' said

Lkimu.

Bezz and Lkimu arrived as Kaq walked out of his wikoum.

'Lkimu, please don't let the girls hear you speak like that. We are the chosen ones; we are honoured. You know this,' said Kaq, 'and Bezz knows this, too.'

'Alas, even though I have the grandest faery blood running hooglejumps through my veins, and know this to be true, I'm with Lkimu with the hopes, Grand Chief.'

'Yes, it is a wonderful world on Mother Earth and we must be full of gratitude for having been gifted this lifetime here, no matter how short,' said Kaq. 'Wherever we go now, Bezz and Lkimu, we carry her with us for eternity.'

'Enough of the long faces,' Kaq's wife reprimanded as she came out of the wikoum. 'We live now. We feast now. We will, we shall and we must. And the Geow-lud-mo-sis-eg await.'

'Let the feast begin,' said Kaq as they all re-entered his home.

Bezz had heard the L'nuk name for the wee folk and thought it lovely. *Their language rings and rolls. And those wee folk. Healers of distinction one and all. For the past three days the stories had flown. And nights. Hector was so fussy that he awoke the whole neighbourhood and the only thing that quietened him was that bonfire in the square.*

'Oh, I was just thinking about our wee bonfire with Hector, Omisseh,' said Bezz to the tallest of the wee folk with the curly orange hair.

Everyone chuckled. It was legend around the village now; Hector likes bonfires in the rain. One of the L'nuk elders said it was well after midnight and pouring 'cats and dogs' when he saw the wee folk laughing around the fire. He said he sort of got a chilly feeling because the fire was apparently not one bit affected by the tons of water coming down on it.

'Ah, yes, we do like our rain fire in the Spring. And now Hector has proven his lineage to our noble race,' laughed Omisseh as he hugged Bezz.

'Oh, Omisseh, you remind me so much of Hector's Da, Gabby. He'd be liking you,' said Bezz.

Omisseh even looked like Gabby, except for the shock of orange hair. Both beings were tall at about four feet high and sported long beards and mischievous smiles. Gabby's hair and beard had turned white centuries before, but Omisseh's remained bright orange. Oddly, the clothing was startlingly similar: red pants and green jackets, caps and shoes. Even the toes were all curled up the same way. Kaq's L'nuk wore only skins and furs, but they had heard of the fine silks from the far East and the cottons and dyes from the far south. Kaq's people loved and revered their healer little L'nuk, and thought of the clothing as a magical possession.

The wee folk could be clearly seen in their garb, when they wanted to be. And then there was the legend about a cloak of mists that granted them invisibility at will.

'The Queen talks about coming over with her Lead Trooper in the future; I look forward to meeting everyone,' said Omisseh. Lowering his voice he added, 'Bezzy, I need some time alone with you.'

'Geewilkertons and frogslegs, I thought you'd never ask,' said Bezz.

'Ah, Bezz, you're a lass,' said a smiling Omisseh. 'We 'Cauns are a funny breed.'

'There t'ain't no t'other,' agreed Bezz. 'How about you come to my place after the Falls and I'll have Lkimu take Mygrth and Hector for a stroll about,' said Bezz.

'How 'bout we ask Kaq beforehand if the two of us can dawdle at the Falls?' said Omisseh.

'Even better. I have a kabillyzillion questions about ol' Ma Earth on Turtle Island,' said Bezz.

'Oh, so I see you've taken a history lesson,' said Omisseh.

'A lesson? Wowseronie. The L'nuk sure know how to teach a girl,' said Bezz.

'They say that Turtle Island is a kabillyzillion times bigger than the Isle of Destiny. Lkimu told me about mountains that touch the sky and fire beaches of sand that go on forever. Have you seen these places, Omisseh?'

Kaq placed his hand on Bezz's shoulder and said:

'Aye, Bezz. He's seen a lot for his wee folk eyes. I know you two must talk, but first let us feast. If you would stay at the Falls after we leave, you'd have a good chance to talk there.'

'Oh! You are psychic. Not two moments ago did I say we should do that very thing? We were going to ask you, Oh Grand Chief!' said Bezz.

'I know,' smiled Kaq. 'I overheard you.'

'Ha. My old friend spies on the likes of the little folk. What in Creation is buzzin' in Creation today, Kaq?' said Omisseh.

The merriment continued on through breakfast, yet there was another tale to be told before the afternoon hike that brought a cloud of sombreness over the village. Omisseh brought a delegate from the inlands to share more ancient words. The young warrior showed no signs of fatigue, although he had traveled far and with a heavy heart. He stood as tall as Kaq and had protective drawings painted on his forearms and chest. He wore a red swatch of animal skin around his stomach that wrapped over his shoulder. His hair was thick, black and plaited. When he sat down, Kaq handed him the carved bone story pipe to begin the sharing ceremony. Kaq spoke first, as was custom, and explained that the warrior, Genawadda, was sent to warn the L'nuk of times to come. Kaq repeated that a good prophecy is one that can be averted before he asked Genawadda to share the eastern story. Genawadda told the gathering that they would face a time of great suffering. They would distrust their leaders and the principles of peace in all the Leagues, and a great white serpent was to come upon the Land of Friendship, and that for a time it would intermingle with the L'nuk serpent as a friend. This serpent would in time become so powerful that it would attempt to destroy the L'nuk, and the serpent would choke the life's blood out of the L'nuk.

He told them that they would be in such a terrible state at this point that all hope would seem to be lost, and he told them that when things looked their darkest a red serpent would come from the north and approach the white serpent, which would be terrified, and upon seeing the red serpent he would release their serpent, who would fall to the ground almost like a helpless child, and the white serpent would turn all its attention to the red serpent. The bewilderment would cause the white serpent to accept the red one momentarily. The white serpent would be stunned and take part of the red serpent and accept him. Then there would be a great argument and a fight. And then the L'nuk would revive and crawl toward the land of the hilly country, and then he would assemble his people together, and they would renew their faith and the principles of peace that had long been established. There would at the same time exist among all people a great love and forgiveness for his brother, and in this gathering would come streams from all over -- not only the Land of Friendship, but from all over -- and they would gather in this hilly country, and they would renew their friendship. They said they would remain neutral in this fight between the white and red serpents.

At the time they were watching the two serpents licked in this battle, a great message would come to them, which would make them ever so humble, and when they become humble, they will be waiting for a young leader, an L'nuk boy, possibly in his teens, who would be a choice seer. Nobody knows who he is or where he comes from, but he will be given great power, and would be heard by thousands, and he would give them the guidance and the hope to refrain from going back to their land and he would be the accepted leader. And they said that they will gather in the land of the hilly country, beneath the branches of an elm tree, and they should burn tobacco and call upon their leader by name when facing the darkest hours, and he will return. They said that as the choice seer speaks to the L'nuk that number as the blades of grass, and he would be heard by all at the same time, and as the L'nuk are gathered watching the fight, they will notice from the south a black serpent coming from the sea, and he is described as dripping with salt water, and as he stands there, he rests for a spell to get his breath, all the time watching to the north to the land where the white and red serpents are fighting. He said that the battle between the white and the red serpents opened very slowly but would then become so violent that the mountains would crack and the rivers would boil and the fish would turn up on their bellies. He said that there would be no leaves on the trees in that area. There would be no grass, and that strange bugs and beetles would crawl from the ground and attack both serpents, and he said that a great heat would cause the stench of death to sicken both serpents.

And then, as the boy seer is watching this fight, the red serpent reaches around the back of the white serpent and pulls from him a hair which is carried toward the south by a great wind into the waiting hands of the black serpent, and as the black serpent studies this hair, it suddenly turns into a woman, a white woman who tells him things that he knows to be true but he wants to hear them again. When this white woman finishes telling these things, he takes her and gently places her on a rock with great love and respect, and then he becomes infuriated at what he has heard, so he makes a beeline for the north, and he enters the battle between the red and white serpents with such speed and anger that he defeats the two serpents, who have already grown battle weary.

When he finishes, he stands on the chest of the white serpent, and he boasts and puts his chest out like he's the conqueror, and he looks for another serpent to conquer. He looks to the land of the hilly country and then sees the L'nuk standing with his arms folded and looking ever so noble that he knows that this L'nuk is not the one to fight. The next direction that he will face will be eastward and at that time a light that is many times brighter than the sun will momentarily blind him. The light will be coming from the east to the west over the water, and when the black serpent regains his sight, he becomes terrified and makes a beeline for the sea. He dips into the sea and swims away in a southerly direction, and shall never again be seen by the L'nuk. The white serpent revives, and he too sees the light, and he makes a feeble attempt to gather himself and go toward that light.

A portion of the white serpent refuses to remain but instead makes its way toward the land of the hilly country, and there he will join the L'nuk with a great love like that of a lost brother. The rest of the white serpent would go to the sea and dip into the sea and would be lost out of sight for a spell. Then suddenly the white serpent would appear again on the top of the water and he would be slowly swimming toward the light. He said that the white serpent would never again be troublesome to the L'nuk. The red serpent would revive and he would shiver with great fear when he sees that light. He would crawl to the north and leave a bloody, shaky trail northward, and the L'nuk would never see him again. He said as this light approaches that their leader would be that light, and he would return to his people. When he returns, the L'nuk would be a greater nation than they had ever been before.

Genawadda sat silently. Kaq's head was reeling from all the news of discord. Another message foreboding times of harrowing change for the people in so short a time, yet as a leader, he would see them through the next shift. He thanked Genawadda and asked everyone to reflect on all they had heard and they would gather again the next morning to call on their ancestors.

After the sharings, the delegation of seven, led by Omisseh, Bezz and Kaq's contingent of five hiked out before the sun was centred in the sky. The ominous words were left behind as the forest became thicker and fewer wikoums were seen. The ever-present sounds of birds lessened. Just as the forest seemed to become a wall of trees and brush, an opening appeared like a portal to another world. Another world indeed. Everyone in the group became silent and only the breaths of the beings and the breaking of twigs or brushing of branches was heard for some time. Bezz thought of her first trip down this very path. *Thank goodness graciousgoddess that Kaq led the way. The branches would rip back fast enough to take an eye out if it weren't for his careful trek through the brush. The smells made you want to lie down on the soft floor of the forest and breathe.*

Ecstasyential. And then the portal. What else could you call the forest wall opening that led to Eden? The sunlight streaming into the dense forest looked like rays of a beacon from Tir-na-nOg. What lay at the end of the trail? The eyes were momentarily blinded coming into the clearing and with the roar of the water, 'twas bedazzling. Everyone turned to the source of the roar and their eyes turned upward. The Falls dropped over 200 feet into a sparkling, crystal clear lake surrounded by huge granite slabs, leftover remnants from the long past Jenu. The hues of greens from trees and brush, purple mosses, diamond waters and the golden glow, all-shimmering in a fine mist. Drawing a deep breath had never seemed so glorious. As everyone entered the clearing, the doorway seemed to disappear and the few beings were in a land that time forgot.

'Look at the birds over there; they are huge,' said Lkimu.

Cranes. Powerful spirit birds.

'And there,' said Omisseh.

Blue Herons.

'It looks so untouched here. What better word to describe a paradise,' said Bezz.

'It doesn't matter how many times I've been here, I still feel humbled and blessed,' said Kaq's wife Naki.

'Today, on the face of this stone, we will celebrate

our Creator. Numi has joined us. She will carve another symbol to remember this day. Numi allows the spirit to enter and she draws what comes,' said Kaq.

'Bezz, Omisseh knows that this symbolizes Creator,' said Kaq as he pointed to the triangle. 'And this is Heaven,' he continued as he indicated the five pointed star. 'Today, we celebrate the alliance of the three crosses, as symbolized here, Bezz; but we shall add another after the ceremony.'

Shadeenok was sitting cross-legged on the largest stone face. He pulled several pouches from his belt and then the beautiful shell.

'Shadeenok. I have a special gift to offer L'nuk today,' said Omisseh as he pulled a red stone from behind his beard. The stone was about three inches in diameter and had a circle hole in the centre.

'Omisseh, is this a ruby?'
'It is what it is. For you, Shadeenok, it is the answer to your future. When all is lost, it will be found. The centre that is missing will be filled and light will shine through and of it,' said Omisseh.

'You speak in riddles I do not understand,' said Shadeenok.

'It is generations away and they will understand. You and I will be anew. For now, I am entrusting the key to you, Shadeenok. Between our worlds, between our peoples, we are the door. When we meet, we will see the pulse and know

108

the time is right. For now, you are the keeper of the ring of creation.'

The other 11 stood in a circle, watching the exchange of the red stone.

'Come and sit in the circle and we begin.'

After the sweet grass ceremony, Kaq asked Omisseh and Bezz to stay behind with Numi while she finished her work. During this trip and a few earlier ones, Bezz noticed many symbols, some worn and ancient looking and some new. Earlier, Numi had sat beside the three crosses symbol and sketched what looked to be a triangle. Bezz and Omisseh moved in to take a better look and Omisseh let out an audible gasp.

'Numi. You've captured my dream.'

The top of the triangle was loped off and the jagged edge was floating in space above an eyeball. The bottom of the triangle was solid on the ground.

'What does it mean, Omisseh?' asked Numi.

'I do not yet know,' said Omisseh, 'but I think I may soon.'

'I did not know this symbol before today. I hope it bodes well for my people,' said Numi, as she began to carve a circle around the symbol.

'Aye, Numi,' said Omisseh. 'Numi, I must take Bezz deeper into the land while you finish your work. If we do not return before that time, please go back to the village without us,' said Omisseh.

'Thank you, Omisseh, I will,' said Numi.

'Oh, and here is a wee satchel for you, Numi. This ochre comes from the south and will stain your hides a deep red. I have more for you. We use this red for our warrior elders,' said Omisseh.

'You honour my people, Omisseh. Thank you,' said Numi.

With a low bow, Omisseh backed up a few steps to join Bezz and they walked over the face of the two slabs toward the waterfall. Halfway up the second slab was a cut in the rock face. The hole appeared to be about two feet long and a foot and a half wide. *I wouldn't have noticed that hole, but for Omisseh slowing me down. I was too preoccupied with the noise and grandeur of the Falls... whewseronie!*

'Here, let me help you, Bezz,' said Omisseh as he guided her onto the rock stairs.

'It's a good thing you slowed me, Omisseh. I've never noticed this hole and I'm surprised no one showed me the other times.'

'The Falls are breathtaking and there is much to notice. Kaq and his people don't come this far normally,' said Omisseh.

'Oh, yes. You're right. We swam in that crystalline lake and danced on the first rock,' said Bezz as she descended the stairs. 'It's quite dark down there, Omisseh.'

'Ha. Going dark is good for the soul, Bezz. That's where you can find the light.'

'Yes, Mother of All. Now tell me there's a lantern down here!' said Bezz.

'You just passed it,' said Omisseh as light flooded around the two faery folk.

'ByZantinecharles! You're one to travel with, with tricks up your sleeves or down your shoes, by Goddess GraciousGod!'

Bezz looked around and noticed the twelve by twenty foot room was solid rock with the same carvings as above ground. Over toward one wall was a pit that had the remnants of a recent fire, by the smell of it all. She looked up to see where the smoke hole was and couldn't see one, even with the light of the lantern. *Lantern? How had Omisseh lit the lantern?* As she looked toward him, she saw another darkened doorway in the opposite corner from where they had entered. *Where does that go?*

'Come,' said Omisseh.

He walked toward the tunnel and turned to Bezz.

'It's okay, Bezz, this is just a decoy.'

'What in Goddess Creation is a decoy?' said Bezz.

111

'Ha. From the old country, are ye lassy? You have a lot to learn,' said Omisseh.

The tunnel was large enough for the wee folk, but Bezz thought Lkimu might have a tough time running through it. He would have to crouch a lot. It ran to the south, away from the Falls and the roar of the water soon turned to a hum and then the tunnel was eerily silent except for the shuffling of their shoes on the rock. They walked in silence for about ten minutes when Bezz noticed a dim light in the distance.

'Here we are, Bezz. Just a little more now.'

The two new friends walked out into a sun-warmed valley, alive with wildlife. Bezz noticed the chirping of the birds in the tunnel but was surprised by both the number and variety of birds in the open valley. There was a light breeze scented with spring flowers and a few clouds dotted the sky. Deer ran together near a forest farther down; others stood nibbling in the grasslands.

'Have you brought me to the other side or The Other Side, Omisseh?' asked Bezz.

'Bezz, I have much to teach in little time. I have shown you this land so you know where it is and how to get here. There are other Little People on Turtle Island. Mine are the Healers. This is the home of the Tricksters. You will meet them, just not yet. They go north in the Spring but return by the Equinox. We have some time. As you can see, you cannot see everything with the naked eye in their land. It seems a utopia or a peaceful paradise. For now, it is. Take a good look around and I will explain later,' said Omisseh.

With that, he turned to re-enter the tunnel that they had come out of only moments before.

'Wait. You mean we can't sit here and chat for a bit, Omisseh?' said Bezz.

Without looking back: 'No, Bezz, come now.'

So many questions. In time, ol' Bezz. Guess I'm getting some good exercise on this side of the pond.

The silence in the tunnel halls gave way to the roar of the Falls. Bezz wasn't too surprised to see Numi sitting in the rock room when they came into the light. She was studiously carving the finishing touches on the broken pyramid-eye symbol near the three crosses symbol on the eastern wall. *What could it all mean?*

'Numi, we will leave you here but we will not yet return to your village. May you go with the flow,' said Omisseh as he started up the stairs.

'Thank you, Omisseh and see you soon, Bezz,' said Numi with hardly a glance at the odd couple.

When they came out by the Falls, Bezz didn't know what to expect, but she didn't expect what happened next. Without a word, Omisseh led her to a path beside the Falls and she saw him jump behind the waterfall. She hesitated and then leapt after him.

Chapter 7: 1550 AD

The Gifts from the

Four Directions

Bezz was hardly wet when she landed behind the Falls.

'What took you so long?' Omisseh said.

'This smells marvelouslous,' Bezz said as she put her hands on her small hips, held her head back and breathed deeply through her nostrils.

'No time to dawdle, Miss Elizabeth Loretta. Follow me,' said Omisseh.

'How did you know my real name?' said Bezz as Omisseh began walking across the solid rock slab.

'Your real name? Oh my, my. You are nubile. I mean numinous,' said Omisseh.

'I heard that, Omisseh!' said Bezz as Omisseh abruptly stopped. She slammed into him as he turned to face the back wall and stuck his hand into a crevice. The rock moved!

'GodGraciousGoddess!' said Bezz.

The two wee folk entered another tunnel with shafts of light streaming in from unseen openings. Bezz didn't notice the gateway silently closing behind them. Before too long, the tunnel opened onto a wide plateau overlooking a real faery tale scene. The azure blue sky was dotted with clouds and spring flowers coloured a meadow with a creek running through it. Omisseh walked westward, toward a giant oak tree, and sat on a rock made for story telling.

'Welcome to The Land That Has No Time, Bezz,' said Omisseh. 'Please, sit.'

'What is this place?' asked Bezz.

'This place is where I will share our story with you. As the leader of the Geow-lud-mo-sis-eg from this side of the pond, I have been given many messages and heard many stories and prophecies over the centuries. On Turtle Island we have many peoples, some of whom I count among my friends. A people named the Navajo call our world the Fourth World and another people named the Hopi call it the Fourth Hoop. Although we come from different cultures, we have learned that we share similar stories and messages,' said Omisseh.

'Many stories talk about how the masculine and feminine imbalance shifts over the millennia. The current cycle began thousands of years ago and now we live in a time of masculine imbalance. Spiritual leaders of the world knew this time was coming. They knew it would be a time when all feminine things would be exploited and destroyed. All Mother Earth cultures, feminine based spirituality and women would be at risk. The spiritual leaders communicated with each other through their intimate connection with Creation and Creator. They decided to hide the sacred and secret teachings because they knew that the two-leggeds, people, would abuse and misuse the teachings. There were many ingenious ways the teachings were hidden: in common words, in story, in song, in art and in geometric patterns found all over the world. In many cases, specific parts of teachings were intentionally forgotten.

These same spiritual leaders knew that the sacred and secret teachings would be made whole again when the two-leggeds healed their hearts. The hearts would be healed when they reconnected with their brothers and sisters from the different directions and colours from around the world. In doing so, they would share their sacred ways with others until the sacred is fully restored.

It is said that there will be a time when the gifts of the four sacred colours, red, white, black and yellow will come together from the Four Directions and combine to create something new that has not been seen since the beginning of time.

It is said that only when beings are open enough in the heart that there will be this deep reconnection that allows a true sharing of the sacred and secret teachings. These teachings from the Four Directions come in the form of the four gifts of sacred elements: earth, air, fire and water.

From the North, the white race masters fire through energy. From energy comes technology comes growth and ultimate understanding of all. The sweet grass you so love is of the North. It represents healing, wisdom and understanding. The braids are of three strands to represent the healing we need to develop: hearts, minds and souls.

From the East, the yellow race masters air through breath. From breath come sounds come healings and ultimate connection to the Divine. All life enters through the Eastern doorway and our lives run in an east to west direction. The great and powerful eagle sits and guards this doorway.

From the West, the red race masters earth through nurturing. From nurturing comes communication comes healing and ultimate healing of Mother Earth. This is the doorway of the Thunderbirds.

From the South, the black race masters water through dance. From dance come rhythms come movements come drummings and then the ultimate harmony of the Universe.

Bezz, we are a part of the shifting world, leading the way into the Fifth. Our destiny is to become 'The Hidden People' until Creator needs us to be seen. Once the world understands that the four sacred colours must blend and flow as one, we shall see the beginnings of our real work. Nothing is created outside until it is created inside first.'

Bezz was so focussed on his words that she didn't move at all when Omisseh stood up.

'This is where you will bring Hector to practice,' said Omisseh.

'Practice?' said Bezz.

'Aye, Acting Ambassador Elizabeth Loretta. Have I stretched your mind a little today?'

'Aye, Grand Chief Omisseh. I'm spinning and wondering if a dragon is going to fly over that water and pluck me away to Kingdom Come,' said Bezz.

'Ha. Bezz, your prowess with Light shows in your eyes. You will be his Light Master Teacher. The Queen has spake. As well, your creationings will begin anew as this temple is your slate. Teachers of other creationings will be at your call. When the time comes, we will be of the fourth world again. The hidden halls are busy with new activities, on this side of the pond and t'other.'

'Creationings? Hidden Halls?' said Bezz.

'Aye. You know some by another name. On your side, Knowth is your Queen's favourite,' said Omisseh.

'Ah. You mean the faery mounds,' said Bezz.

She thought of the whale shaped mounds that had been built so long ago. As a wee, wee one, Bezz had been awed by the underground palaces. She remembered running errands with her own mother as a child and then later as the Queen's aide. Mostly, Bezz remembered never wanting to leave the enchanted world.

So, they have them here, too.

'Is this place a gateway to one?' asked Bezz.

'No, no. But there is a similar opening to our main Hallway, far inland. From above, the fields of tear shaped drumlins go on forever, but the Great Hallway was built near connecting ley lines in the middle of seven hills in a land named the kawarthas. We will travel there when Hector grows,' said Omisseh. 'For now, we must prepare Kaq's peoples.'

I well remember Knowth. Ma said they built it over 5000 years ago. Same as Newgrange and Dowth. Ma said they were sacred intersections for the Queen.
I never did understand, even when I'd go with the Queen.

120

'You call them 'tear shaped drumlins', but on t'other side, we think of them as whale shaped, Omisseh,' said Bezz.

'We have seen much, Bezz. Soon almost all of the races will forget their purpose. Even the folk that travel from your Land of Destiny will forget their celtic roots. Who could have thought that? Someone from Ireland, Scotland or Wales forgetting? Even more astounding, some will deny our Creator. As the fifth race, the Creator has given us the honour of being the Keeper of Mother Earth. Kaq knows this. Others around the world know this. As stewards of the earth, we are preparing for the coming of the fifth world, a world of harmony and balance,' said Omisseh.

'I have heard seers on the other side and they speak of this and Hector's role. I am humbled and honoured to be here with you, Omisseh, and to be a part of all,' said Bezz.

'Together, Bezz, we will enjoy the fifth world of peace and abundance, as we will become of the earth and all her glories.'

I am not afraid of any of this. I will share my life with him. I am blessed.

As Bezz was thinking, Omisseh stood and swooped toward the oak. Some birds flew up to the branches, whistling and a few animals appeared nearby, grazing. She smiled as he turned and opened his hand, revealing a glowing ruby.

'Aye, Bezz, I was thinking the same thing,' said Omisseh.

While Omisseh and Bezz were plotting their new course, Omisseh's people were working with Kaq to ready the villagers for the devastation to come. All of Omisseh's little people had wanted to come to say goodbye to Kaq and the others in the confederacy, but it was decided to send the delegation of seven so preparations could commence immediately. No one spoke of tomorrow; everyone worked at assigned tasks, concentrating on going through the process.

'Lkimu, I wonder if you'll ever get to see my home?' said Myrgth as she fed Hector.

'Myrgth, let us enjoy now. Tell me about your home,' said Lkimu.

'Well, I grew up in Clew Bay, right near St. Patrick's Cragh. It's a glorious mountain, Lkimu. My folks call it St. Patrick's, because they loved that man so, but a few hundred years ago everyone knew it as Eagle Mountain,' said Myrgth.

'Eagle. A powerful totem,' said Lkimu.

'I come from a magical place. Even before King Oberon, there was King Midir. That song you like that I sing to Hector is called *The Wooing of Etain*. King Midir was known as the 'Very Proud One' who dwelt at the fairy mound of Bri-Leith. He was married to Etain the Goddess but she fell in love with the King Eochaid of Ireland and ran away to marry him,' said Myrgth.

122

'Faery King and Goddess? That King of Ireland must have been someone special,' said Lkimu.

'Aye. They say he was near seven feet tall, with flowing curls about him. Goddess Etain had seen his inner light shining from across the bog of Lamrach, and even though happily married to the faery king, she travelled to see who carried her twin flame. It is said that when Etain and Eochaid first saw each other, that there were thunderous crashes from on high during a blizzard of snow. All the while, Midir looked on and tried to woo her back. Etain loved her old husband, but she stayed at Castle Eochaid, unable to leave what peace she had found there. After a time, King Midir followed and challenged King Eochaid to a game of chess. Eochaid knew then that he had lost his love. Nobody could turn down this request or win against a fairy King. Knowing this, King Eochaid asked King Midir to perform several tasks when he lost the game of chess. He asked the faery king to build a causeway across the bog of Lamrach, so he could cross the bog and see Etain the Goddess from time to time. Remember the words to the song, Lkimu? It goes like this:

Pile on the soil; thrust on the soil;
Red are the oxen around who toil;
Heavy the troops that my words obey;
Heavy they seem, and yet men are they
Strongly, as piles, are the tree-trunks placed:
Red are the wattles above them laced:

Tired are your hands, and your glances slant;
One woman's winning this toil may grant !
Oxen ye are, but revenge shall see;
Men who are white shall your servants be;
Rushes from Teffa are cleared away
Grief is the price that the man shall pay:
Stones have been cleared from the rough Meath
ground;
Where shall the gain or the harm be found?
Thrust it in hand! Force it in hand!
Nobles this night, as an ox-troop stand;
Hard is the task that is asked, and who
From the bridging of Lamrach shall gain, or rue?'

As Myrgth finished the song, Little Hector finished
eating and held out his arms to her.

'I could listen to you sing forever, Myrgth,'
said Lkimu. 'That was beautiful. I didn't understand it, but
you make the words ring.'

'If we had several lifetimes, I think it would
be hard to explain the faery realm to a mortal, Lkimu. We are
a good race and enjoy many blessings,' said Myrgth as she
bounced and played with Hector on the bearskin rug.

'My home is in many places. On your world,
I visit the Celtic homes of Ireland, Scotland and Wales for
my work; but we have worlds within worlds, Lkimu. The
Celts call our invisible world Magh Mell. If you see one of us
around water, like a stream or a lake, and we disappear, that
means we've crossed to the land of Magh Mell, the plain of

124

honey. My favourite is Tir na nOg, the land of eternal youth. You'll love it there. Then there's Tir Tairngiri, the land of promise. What's lovelier than a promise? Oh, they're all so special. The silver cloud plain is called Magh Argatonel… I remember another mortal song about us… one of them visited the fairy realm of Mag Mell. Laegaire mac Crimthainn. Do you want to hear it?' asked Myrgth.

'Myrgth, your voice reminds me of your land of promise. Please sing and let me play with Hector while you do,' said Lkimu.

White shields they carry in their hands,
With emblems of pale silver;
With glittering blue swords,
With mighty stout horns.
In well-devised battle array,
Ahead of their fair chieftain,
They march amid blue spears
Pale visage, curly headed bands
They scatter the battalions of the foe
They ravage every land they attack
Splendidly they march to combat
A swift, distinguished, avenging host !

No wonder though their strength be great:
Sons of queens and kings are one and all;
On their heads are
Beautiful golden-yellow manes.

With smooth comely bodies,

With bright blue-starred eyes,
With pure crystal teeth,
With thin red lips.

Good they are at man-slaying,
Melodious in the ale-house,
Masterly at making songs,
Skilled at playing chess.

'Ha. Not a love song, that one,' said Lkimu. 'Are the faeries known as man-slayers across the waters?'

'I just wanted to see if you were paying attention. Those songs are hundreds of years old; the Celts have had their eyes and hearts opened. Some of their kings and queens have been honoured with the knowing of Mag Mell,' said Myrgth.

'My Queen Myrgth, I honour you now with the knowing of Mother Earth cedars and pines. Let's take Hector to the forest so we can breathe in her trees,' said Lkimu as he handed Hector to Myrgth.

Myrgth stood and gently touched Lkimu's shoulder and the unlikely trio disappeared from the wikoum.

PART TWO

...help arrives

Chapter 8

Old Mother Shipton's

Buried Treasure

My great, great, great, great, great, great Grandma was a witch. A real witch. Everybody in our family had forgotten the old days, but I found Grandma Witch's old diary. Her name was Ursula. When she got older, nobody called her that. She said it kind of made her sad. Everyone was afraid of her because she knew things that were going to happen before they even happened. They called her Old Mother Shipton.

She knew I was going to find her diary. She said she thought it would help me, so she dug the hole herself. Just for me. It all started when I found a key hanging on a nail in the attic. The key had my name engraved on it. When I showed it to my Mom, she said that Dad had bought a box of old kitchen stuff at an auction and the key was in it. That was before I was born. Mom liked the look of the antique key, but had long forgotten the name engraved on it when I found it. I thought it was freaky, but I kept the key in the night table drawer beside my bed and pulled it out to look at when I was really missing Daddy.

I was digging in the backyard with my friends, pretty close to the old oak tree. We kept digging up white quartz crystal rocks. We thought they were prettier than diamonds. Mom said they weren't worth any money, but they'd bring good energy to the old tree. The boys lived a few doors down, Angus and Tom, and they were really good diggers. I was a tomboy, so I was pretty good, too. Their older brother Thor used to play with us, but he was a teenager like their sister Ruby, so we had to find a new friend. We were digging a hole to China to make new friends. It was a pretty big hole. I don't know why we picked that spot to dig. We could've dug anywhere. Maybe because it wasn't so hot in the shade there.

I hit the top of the box with the shovel and knew it wasn't a rock. My friends knew it, too. It took us about two hours of solid digging to get that old wooden box out of the ground. It must have been a hundred pounds, with the wood and stuff inside. We saw the lock on the side and I told them that I had the key. They were freaked because they knew I never lied. I ran into the house and didn't say a word to Mom.

Click. After being buried for hundreds of years, the key still made a click when I turned it. It took two of us to pry open the lid. There it was. Two books, a satchel and a crystal rod wrapped in golden wires and topped with a huge purple stone. We found out later that the purple stone was called an amethyst. Said it was a healing wand. It said so in her diary. Oh ya, the two books. One was her diary and the other one was a book of spells. That's what it said: *Book of Spells*.

Inside the front cover, when we worked up the nerve to open it, it said, 'January 1, 1555, London, England. Ye who read these words be forewarned. This *Book of Spells* is Mother Shipton's *Book of Spells*. Ye must know that this book is intended for one person only. If ye be Lucy Kelly, then read on. If ye be any other living soul, ye be wise to bury me where ye found me and forget all about me.'

The hairs on my arms stood straight up. That's when Angus and Tom said they had to go home for lunch. I knew they were lying, though, because their mother was my Mom's best friend, Mary Hickey. She'd let them play until they were hungry and not get mad. AND they didn't even ask me to split the money or gems with them. Oh ya, the satchel. Grandma Witch knew I'd be born at a time when 'thoughts would fly around the world in the twinkling of an eye'. She said I might need some coins and gems if one of her friends didn't show up, so she told me to look in the satchel and trade it in for money. That kind of scared me. Still, I lay on the grass reading her diary until I heard Ma call me for supper. By then, I had decided two things. I would show Ma the wooden box, the *Book of Spells* and the satchel right away, but I was saving Grandma Witch's diary and the crystal wand for another time.

~ The Hidden Scroll ~

Two hours later, the table unset and the chicken untouched and cooled on the stovetop, Mom and I lay talking on her bed. Dad had been dead for years, and the two of us were real close. I was starting to feel guilty about not telling her about the diary and the wand and was just about to tell her when she let out a yelp.

'Lucy, there's something tucked in behind the back cover.'

How did I miss that? It was because I'd been so fascinated by the diary. It wasn't really a diary, it was more like a love letter to me. Even when we were looking at *The Spell Book*, I kept thinking about what Grandma said. She said she was going to teach me how to change her prophecy. I didn't have time to google the word yet and couldn't ask Mom.

'What is it?'

'I think it's a scroll,' Mom said as she pulled out a tightly wrapped ream of paper. It was quite long, almost a foot. *The Spell Book* itself was several inches longer, but the paper was made out of something different. Ma had said we'd have to be very careful and take it to a museum so we could make sure the paper wouldn't disintegrate. The black leather looked in good shape. Pretty awesome to see that someone had burnt the letters S-P-E-L-L B-O-O-K in some kind of old fancy printing. Must have been Grandma Witch herself.

'I'm afraid to unroll it, Lucy.'

'Just do it, Ma. The suspense is killing me!' We sure didn't look like two witches lying on that bed. Mom had always worn her hair long and curly, and the rest of her didn't look like any old crag. When she smiled, you could see Heaven in her big brown eyes. She always had been a real good athlete, and still liked playing basketball and swimming and was a graceful dancer, too. She was just perfect and when she called me 'Mini Me', I'd smile and think I wasn't even close. There was an excitement in her eyes that I hadn't ever seen. We were having fun. As she unfurled the paper, I saw that word. Prophecy.

'Ma! What does that mean?'

Her face changed to a worried look and she stopped unraveling the scroll.

'Maybe we'd best wait until we talk to the museum, doll.'

'Ma. What does prop-whatever mean?'

She knew I had a stubborn streak a mile wide because I'd inherited it from her. She said that was one of my lessons to learn for this life. I didn't know about that, but I did know I wasn't going to wait a second longer. I went for the dictionary. Thank God I had a reason! She knew where I was going and didn't stop me. I knew that it wasn't because she knew that I was stubborn that she let me go. I knew it was to give her time to read whatever Grandma Witch had written.

We kept the dictionary on the sideboard near the kitchen table. I remembered how to spell the word and looked it up quickly. It read: prophecy: 'a prediction of future events'. Hmm. I yelled up the stairs as I was climbing them: 'Is it a scary prediction, Ma?'

'It's meant for you. Here, you read it out loud to me.'

'Prop…'

'Oh. Prof-e-see.'

'Okay. Prophecy.

Prophecy

Centuries will come and centuries will go
And Mother Earth will let you know
She'll tell you to stop your wasteful ways
She'll help guide you to more holy days

Iron ships will cross the pond,
Above, below, they will go on
Land will see criss-crossing too
And Sky will not be spared by you
Cracks in earth and cracks in sky
Will lead to Ma Earth's woeful cry

There will be no time to sigh
Mountains will tear and crumble fine
Oceans will rise, tis all a sign
Men will forget their bloody fights
And run to homes with no lights
All will seek the God they knew
And Goddess, too, in multitude

Where life had long been lost to greed
The greedy came to a time of need
Fortunes lost, no food, no water
Here comes Mother Shipton's daughter
Before the curse of greed come true
There is but one chance and that is you
Lucy Kelly, read and learn
Your heart is true, you will not burn

There are some in your time that see
That love guides all through eternity
You shall find them, if you seek
You will find them in the meek

Guide your Mother, she does forget
You lift the veil and destiny is met!
Then together we three shall shred these words
And have turned around all with love's own sword.

Wow. We'll have to re-read it a few thousand times, hey, Ma. How can she expect me to guide you? And what does THAT mean, 'we three'?!'

'Well, Lucy. There are two expressions that came into my mind. First, 'out of the mouths of babes' and that means that young people see everything in a fresh, new perspective. And second, 'A great prophecy is an unfulfilled prophecy'. I heard that one a long time ago and thought it was some kind of cop out because it means that the prediction never happened. I've read some prophecies in the Bible and Nostradamus. Some of William Blake's stuff, too, but I never heard of Mother Shipton. Let's google her. I love what she says about love. You know I think we live in a love world and that we're screwing it up somehow. You're right. We'll read it over. She doesn't give us much to go on.'

Honestly, I wanted to tell her about the diary but I couldn't get a word in edgewise. Ma was like that sometimes and I inherited it from her. I was just going to tell her about the diary when her cell phone rang.

I looked back at the 'we three' line while Ma picked up the phone. Can you imagine finding a 500-year-old book of spells, an ancient prophecy and a bag of riches and then talking on the phone for an hour about silly stuff? I was so excited that I had to go on to Ma's computer, but I could still hear her conversation with Mary Hickey. At first I thought Mary, she made all the kids call her by her name, was calling because of the boys being scared, but as I listened, I knew they were talking about some of their friends.

'I know she can seem rotten sometimes, but whenever you start to think that, just bite your tongue and say 'cancel that thought', Mary, and replace that nasty thought with a lovely, warm thought about something else. Every time, Mary. Soon, you won't be thinking anything negative at all.'

I had to stop listening so I could concentrate. There. Cancel that voice out of my head. For now.

Mother Shipton's Cave? What is this?

'Mom, you've got to see this. Now.'

'Sorry, Mary. I'm helping Lucy now. I'll call you later, alligator. Just remember, think positive!' She came running down and stood by my side.

'Ma, she's real.'

'Of course she is, Lucy. What, you believe an Internet site and not a 500 year old book?'

'Ha. It says she was so ugly when she was born. You must take after her.'

'No, that was you.'

'Hey. Her husband's name was Tony. Grandpa Tony. I like it. That's where we get our Italian from, hey Ma. An Irish spaghetti lover. Oh. She was born in Knaresborough, England. How did she get across the Atlantic Ocean 500 years ago? Look. It says she never had any children. We'll have to read her di…'

Honestly, I was just going to tell Ma about the diary when there was a knock at the door.

~ Ursula Lives ~

'Were you expecting Angus?' said Joan as she started for the front door.

'No, Ma. Maybe it's Mr. Bogeyman. Ooo. Aah,' said Lucy.

Joan saw the shadow of the little person through they opaque window and opened the door. It wasn't Angus.

'Ah. I was looking for Mary Hickey, but I see I've come to the wrong house,' said the odd looking little man. 'Sorry to bother you, Ma'am.'

'Oh, that's okay. Mary lives three doors down that way,' said Joan, pointing.

'Did your Ma ever tell you it's impolite to point, lassy?'

'Aye, she did, and will ye ever forgive me?' Joan shot right back.

'Ha. After I finish my business with Mary, I'll be back to see you. Expect me,' said Ambassador Hector before he turned and sauntered down the steps.

'Ah, okay,' said Joan.

'Who is it, Ma?'

She had shut the door before she had thought to ask him his name. She opened it and the wee man was nowhere to be seen. Not on the sidewalk, nor the lawns. *Where did he go? It was only a second ago that I shut that door! I'm going to phone Mary back.*

'Ah, it was someone looking for Mary Hickey, babe,' said Joan.

'Why do you look so weird? Was it a man?' asked Lucy.

'Kind of. I mean, yes. He was so short. And he had on the weirdest outfit. If I didn't know better, I'd say a gnome just knocked at our front door.'

'What do you mean, a gnome?'

'You know. Remember the stories I used to read to you about faeries and elves? There were gnomes, too. You know. Like the statue gnomes you see on front lawns.'

'Oh. You mean like the seven dwarfs or something?'

Before Joan had moved or had time to answer, there was a second knock. Joan could see the same little shadow. She opened the door.

'Ah me, ah my. It seems that Mary's out with her brood. Would you be kind enough to invite a wee lad in for a spell?' asked Hector.

Joan was obviously startled by the word 'spell' and turned to see Lucy stop in her tracks. Both of the Kelly girls looked at the table, thinking they'd brought the *Spell Book* down from upstairs. It was safe in the bedroom.

'Sure. Please come in, but I just got off the phone from Mary... Lucy, would you get Mr. Ah...' said Joan.

'No, the name's Hector, not Ah,' said Hector with a smile.

'Mr. Hector, would you like a cup of tea or a glass of water?' said Lucy.

'Please, call me Hector. Let's just see what you can conjure up, Lucy,' he said with a mischievous smile.

Hector was having fun with the girls. Lucy had long been a favorite of his and he often asked her guardian for updates. He knew all about the treasure trove because he'd been with Ursula when she buried it. Finding it now was synchronistic, of course. Lucy was still young, but not too young. Joan was ready for it all. Her husband, Freddy, had been dead for a few years; it was time for the girls to get on with living.

139

'Are you a friend of Ursula's?'

Quite intuitive, lassy.

Yes, I am.

'Who is Ursula, Lucy?' asked her mom.

'She was your Great, Great, Great, Great, Great, Great Grandma, Joan.'

'Is he talking about Mother Shipton?' said Joan, looking at Lucy, stunned.

'None other,' said Hector. 'A beauty inside and out. She had the crowning glory of a goddess, curls to no end. You actually remind me of the young Ursula, Joan. Has she never gotten through to you in all your years?'

'Oh my. Sometimes I hear a voice and I know it's not mine. I guess I was afraid to hear her,' said Joan.

'Fear is that nasty fiend. When fear wells up, you must shine your heart light and feel the waves of love. Remember, from the very first breath in human form, you switch on the fears of rejection, betrayal, abandonment, and loneliness and on and on. Whatever either of you fear now, please understand that you must deal with it and it will be gone. It's between being scared and being sacred. Sacred/scared. See? You know sacred means 'whole' of course, as we are all one. Lesson one done.'

'Wow. Hector.'

'Wow, Joan.'

'I heard that!'

'Mom! You heard that?'

'Girls, girls. You must make a pot of tea. Or better yet, give ol' Hector a wee dram of the nectar of the gods and he'll forever be your friend.'

'Mom. He wants a beer,' said the eleven year old intuitive.

'Ah, yes. I have a beer. I will get you a beer. I will get me some scotch. A big one,' said Joan as she mumbled to herself on the way to the kitchen.

'Joan, come on back. I was only joking. It's okay. The party is on me today.'

As she turned, Joan saw a lovely nook table appear with drinks for all. Also on the table were a few little platters of vegetables and snacks.

'A treat, no tricks,' said Hector. 'Any questions anyone?'

'I have a few, but would like to start with the Mary Hickey thing. Why did you say you were going to visit her when you first came?'

'I was. And I did. She's waiting for the boys at the YMCA and she phoned you from her cell.'

'Oh. But I mean, if you're here about Ursula and telling us she was our Grandma, then why did you go to Mary Hickey's?'

She's involved, too, Mom.

How?

Hector?

'Don't you two catch on fast? As a matter of fact, I've been working at the Hickey's and had to prepare them for the next adventure before I made contact with ye.'

'What adventure?'

'We'll get to that. Right now, I want to catch you up on what they know. Yes, they. Mary and her entire family are now earthen ambassadors for the King and Queen of Faery. King Oberon and Queen Titiana have decided to renew their friendship with the earthen peoples. I am Ambassador Hector Grodstooth of the P.L.A.C.E. on official business to awaken the Kellys, namely, yoursElves. Are you ready?'

'Is it going to hurt?'

'Wait, do me first!' said Joan.

'Ha. Ha. Girls, girls. You are too funny.'

'Ye must know your purpose? Do you never go dark?'

He means when we connect, Ma.

'No, lass. It's more than that. It's to know where ye come from and where ye go from there. It is the knowing who ye are.'

'I tell Lucy that no one knows why we're here, but we have each other and a lifetime to be kind to each other and figure it out. We always pray a lot, Hector,' said Joan.

'I'm one of the answers to your prayers. I've been sent to ready you for your Grandmama.'

'What do you mean, Hector?'

'There's that prophecy you found. There was another one that you haven't. When Ursula saw the big picture, she wasn't sure of how things would turn out, with free will and all… so she thought she might need your help. And who better to help than hersElf?'

'Are you trying to tell us that Old Mother Shipton is coming here from 500 years ago?'

'In a manner of speaking, yes,' said Hector.

'She'll be a sight by now, Ma.'

'Aye. But you'll be seeing her rainbow. She'll come when ye know how to ask her and she'll come as a voice to ye. A voice through the ages. As we all do, she exists as her soul and it has been written that she will return in voice form to help those who have forgotten to awaken the subconscious to the shifting world. Those are in words you'll understand, Joan. Lucy here is young enough to still feel the connection to Mother Earth and Spirit. She knows we are all manifestations of Creator and her knowing knows we are all one. In this knowing, she understands that Mother Earth longs for peace; too long has humankind been tearing at her heart. Ursula was a gifted seer and seeker of her time and she has been working and helping others in Spirit. She prophesized the coming of Lucy in her bloodline and made a pact to help with the Earth Changes of our times.'

143

'Ma. Remember when I said I thought I was here to heal the bloodlines?'

'Oh ya. I thought you were creepy that day. You were five or six. You got head lice at school and were so mad at God,' said Joan as she turned to Hector. 'She asked me why God invented lice and I told her that I didn't know, but maybe lice was good for animals and just bad for people. She started to cry and said, 'No, Ma. It's just bad. I don't know why God would make something so bad. I used to think God looked like a rainbow and now I think she looks like a bug!' *She?* I said, 'What?' And then I looked at her with tears streaming down her face and didn't say anything more. Later that night, she said God told her that she was here to heal the bloodlines. I didn't know what to say, so I just hugged her.'

Hector stood and put his arms high in the air and said, "And that, my dear girls, is exactly what has gone wrong here on God's Green Earth. Why didn't you say something to the child? Children need to talk about what goes on inside them,' Hector was passionate and thumping at his chest. 'It's no good to come onto Mother Earth and be of Mother Earth and not discuss her. We are all God's children. Each and every one of us, yet we don't teach our children how to go quiet and listen? We're too busy filling their wee heads with facts and rules to take any notice of what Creator has taught. Using all of your senses to feel a part of all of creation with the Creator. No more illusion of separateness. One of your wee artists, Akiane, said 'I broke down all conclusions into illusions and confusions'. We had a great laugh at her astuteness when she said that at the tender age of 12. You'd do well to google her, Lucy, and see some of her other truths. My favorite of hers is: 'Destiny is a target. God is a bow. The soul is an arrow.' I want you to think about that one, girls. I'll give you a pop quiz on it someday soon. See what happens when you get me going? Now, where was I? Ah. My old friend Ursula. You must know that I helped her with the treasure chest, Lucy?'

'Are you saying you know what was in it?'

'Aye, the Hickey boys told me.'

'Serious?' Lucy hadn't seen Angus or Tom since they ran home. She knew them and figured they'd be coming back for the loot after they got over their fear.

'Ha, no. Lucy, I know what was in it because I gave Ursula the chest and I was there when she filled it up! It was her only trip to the mainland. She'd had visions of America, but 'twas our Queen Titiana that arranged for her to come and see for herself. She loved it so here, but had to return to The Isle of Destiny. It had been written.'

'Ma…' started Lucy, but Hector interrupted.

'Forgive me for interrupting your train of thought, wee lass, but I must tell ye another bit about Ursula before I forget. She was a very private lady. Do not talk too much about her to anyone.'

Lucy knew that Hector wanted her to keep the diary to herself. Intuitively, he had corroborated parts of the story she had read in the diary that afternoon. Ursula loved Titiana and Titiana had taught her in the way of the faery, so she never had any material needs. But it was her kinfolk and neighbors that were the blight of her existence. Ursula did not have a whit of karma about her, and she had signed on to help out a considerable number of folk back then. Every realm was praying and hoping for the return of the Golden Age of legend, the Age where everyone, every animal and every thing lived in peace and knew love was the All. For some, the 1500s were a time of hope and exploration, inner and global.

Ursula's human circle just did not get it. They ridiculed her for her predictions. They shunned her for her talk of healing. They gossiped and ruined her reputation. The years took their toll and when her beloved Tony died, it was the worst of times. Ursula thought their little Zelda would have a better life in another town with some distant cousins. Ursula traveled to Eagle Mountain in Ireland and left her old life and Zelda behind. For a long while, she'd 'talk' to Zelda, but then realized it was confusing the young girl. Ursula visited her from time to time and followed her bloodline through the ages. Her gift allowed for that. She kept to herself after giving up Zelda, but enjoyed her faery friends and her travels to possible future lands. When the Queen

146

asked Ursula to travel to the mainland to meet Hector, she was thrilled. She could read other people like a book, but when it came to her own life, little was revealed. She prepared for months, knowing that her bloodline was destined to continue on the mainland.

'I remember the first time I saw your Grandma. If I recall correctly, she came in on a ship named the Brown Robin and had an uneventful voyage. Still, over thirty days at sea is enough to knock a good sea-faring man to his knees, what with scurvy and storms and all. I stood on the beach with Omisseh and Kaq. The scouts had alerted us that the tall ship was arriving. It was near sundown and a mild day in May. Ursula started waving as soon as she saw our group. Her hair was a cascade of auburn curls, blowing in the breeze. The sun behind her made her aura glow like an angel's. And that smile. Ah, the memory.'

'So, this was like 500 years ago?'

'Yes Ma'am, t'was.'

'Om something and Kack?'

'Ah, so much to tell. Ye'd best see it firsthand.'

With that, Hector, Joan and Lucy were standing in an enormous cavern. As far as the eye could see, there were forty-foot high oval columns each playing a moment in history. It was too much for the girls to fathom. Lucy focused on one, hoping to glean some kind of understanding as to the meaning. It looked like hieroglyphs. Her eyes moved to the next. It looked like a scene from an Arctic play day; the northern lights shimmering in the background while the children sledded down a hill. Joan pulled at her arm.

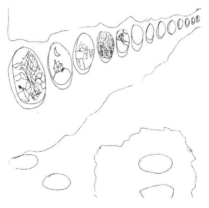

'Look, Lucy'

It was Joan. But it wasn't. Ursula. Sitting on a rock, her feet in the water and holding her baby's head while soaping it. A man came into view, smiling.

'Urse the Nurse. I'm finished at the market. Let's take Z and go upstream a ways and have a picnic.'

'Aye, Tony. If you'd grab the cheese and bread, I'll finish up here and we'll be gone.'

He leaned down and kissed her and was gone from sight. Ursula turned and looked directly at us.

'Yes, that be Tony. My sweet, brave Tony. Hector can teach you how to come to visit me here by the water. Anytime you need me, I'll be here.'

The scene faded and she was gone. Next appeared a view of a street scene with Ursula walking and carrying Zelda, smiling and cooing at her. The rows of houses on either side were well kept and people were milling about, talking and busy with daily chores. The peaceful, sunny day was shattered by a scream. Everyone stopped.

'Tony!' Ursula clutched Zelda tightly and ran, her skirts flying behind her.

As she rounded the corner, a small crowd was gathering. She didn't notice the cheese and bread strewn to the side. She only saw Tony, her Tony, blood streaming from his head. She knew people were talking to her, but she couldn't hear their words. Her Tony. She knew he was gone, but she cradled his head in her lap. Her baby cried. She cried.

Joan and Lucy were crying. As empaths, they felt her anguish.

'What happened to him, Hector?'

The next scene had started. Ursula was lying on her bed sleeping with her baby.

Hector and the girls were back in the Kelly's living room.

'It was a long time before I found out. That was the start of the uprisings. Gifted people like Ursula were persecuted. One of her greatest persecutors was from a family that had owed Tony's family a great deal over a land dispute. Tony was not directly involved, but the Upshed fellow had snuck up on him and bashed his head with a rock. Dead before he hit the ground. The murderer claimed he was doing everyone a favor because the Shipton witches were going to bring blight on the town. He actually got off on all charges, even though the witness, whose scream you heard, told everyone about the cowardly deed. Times were different then. Even though the neighbors loved Tony and Ursula, they turned their backs on the young couple when the tides turned. It's not something Ursula will talk about.'

'What was that place you took us?'

'The Hall of Fame, we call it.'

'Is everything recorded? Everything?'

'Is that like the Akashic Records?'

'Tis what it tis; Tis a place for you to talk to your Grandmama.'

'You said we'd learn about Om and Kack.'

'Funny thing about those Halls, whoever runs them has a mind of their own. Sometimes, I go looking for something and learn about something else, just like now.'

'Om was Omisseh and he was the Leader of the Wee Folk on this side and Kaq was Chief Kaqtukwow of L'nuk of the Mi'kmaq Nation on the east coast. When I arrived in Canada, as a babe in arms, I was the designate Ambassador for the Little People. Times on this side of the pond were even crazier. The Europeans were fighting over land that the natives had enjoyed for over 10,000 years as their home. The

English, French and Spanish explorers brought death to these shores. All of this had been prophesized by many of the indigenous cultures over the Earth. Omisseh and the King and Queen of Faery decided to go underground and Kaq and his people were involved. It is said that there is a common thread that runs through all indigenous folks and it was this commonality that the three peoples were attempting to preserve.'

'Was it our connection to Spirit?'

'Ah, wee Lucy; ye are ye Grandma's daughter.'

Chapter 9

Revisiting the Hall

of Fame

'Angus told me about the Wishing Well, Hector,' said Lucy.
'He thought you'd have given Mom and me one. Why didn't
you?'

They were sitting in Lucy's backyard, the gnome and
the girl. If you glanced from the road, you could see them
having a tea party. Hector said he'd rather have a wee pint,
but Lucy insisted he try her freshly baked coconut oatmeal
cookies and they wouldn't go well with beer. He took a bite
of the cookies and his eyebrows rose in surprise.

'Remarkable. You sure can bake, Lucy.'

'Hector.'

"For goodnessgraciousgoddessakes, Lucy. You must
know you don't need a wishing well?' said Hector.

'Well, I would like to wish for a few things when
you're not around, Hector. Mostly stuff I don't really need,
but would love to have. You know, girl stuff.'

'Lucy, Lucy. Do you know that if a person is sick and
puts a magnet under his bed that he'll be cured?'

'What are you talking about Hector?'

'I'm saying, if you think you will be cured, you will be cured. The magnet acts as a catalyst.'

'Listen, Hector. I'm not sick. I don't need a magnet. I want a Wishing Well!'

'Lucy. Learn to listen. Listen to learn. If you want something, it means you're lacking it, right? So get that word out of your head. If you wish a wish, you desire that wish and ye shall get that wish. But it has always been about knowing. If you believe in something, it's because someone told you to believe it. Faith comes from knowing. You don't need a Wishing Well because you are the Wishing Well.'

'Oh, Hector. Mom does this to me sometimes! If the Queen doesn't want me to have a Wishing Well here, I can go over and use the one at Angus'.'

Hector jumped up. Off the chair, he shrank considerably beside Lucy.

'Come with me, you young whippersnapper,' said Hector.

Lucy followed Hector in through the back door to the living room. Lucy and Joan's house had been transformed as well.

'See this tile here,' Hector said as he placed his foot on a marble tile beside the piano. There was an empty space between the piano and the wall.

'Yes.'

'Put your foot where mine was,' Hector said as he moved out of Lucy's way.

'OK.'

'Make your wish.'

'But there's no Wishing Well,' she said as she put her tippy toes on the tile.

'Make your wish,' an exasperated Hector commanded.

'Um. I wish I had a new… Um. A new. I know. A new bathing suit!'

Instantly, a lime green shorts-like bottom bathing suit with black trim and an open backed, halter style polka-dotted top of the same colours, appeared.

It's out of *Now Girl's* new spring swimsuit issue. It's my favourite one, Hector.'

'Okeedokey. Let's get back to yOur cookie fest,' said Hector.

'You did that,' Lucy said, following Hector.

'If you say so.'

"I say so.'

'Hector, can we go back to the Hall of Fame Hall place? Just you and me.'

'Lucy, you know your Mom asked that she be there if we go to the Halls," said Hector. 'She won't be back until suppertime, so you'll have to wait.'

'Please, Hector?'

'Well, since you said the magic word. But first, why? What is it you're looking for?'

'Well, I don't want my Mom to get sad, but I'd like to go and look at some of Dad's life. You know, when he was young and happy.'

'Oh, sweetum cakes. I see your Mama knows more than I in her young years. How 'bout you hold off on that thought and we'll talk to your Mom about it. I'll take you in for a historical moment that I know your Mama won't mind,' said Hector.

It was only Lucy's second time in the Halls but she knew it would always remain astonishing and wondrous for her or for any visitor. Somehow its grandeur was intimidating, but her natural curiosity spurred her to look past Hector.

'It's like a movie library. But real life. So cool,' said Lucy as she noticed the elephant herd splashing in the muddy river on one 'screen'. Right next to the elephants, a nighttime scene of people scurrying about on a large downtown street played out.

'Oh, so cool. There's no volume until you look at the oval. But what is the order in here, Hector? Like, how would I find Dad? It seems to be so random?'

'Here's the one you must see, Lucy,' Hector said as he pointed to the oval in front of him.

155

Lucy hadn't noticed what he was looking at. She looked quickly to the oval and back to Hector's face. There were tears in his eyes. She looked back and gasped.

'Hector. I've never seen them.'

'The Northern Lights. That's what you know them as, but the wee folk call them by another name. My Grandma Glory was a friend of your Grandma Ursula and they were both vision seekers. Somehow, together they travelled to see the Northern Dancing Skylights… nodas… and many of their greatest visions came from those sacred journeys.'

'They are so beautiful. Listen. I can hear them sway.'

'You have the gift, Lucy. Most cannot hear a sound. You become as one with the nodas and the nodas will gift you with messages.'

'Hector. It's like music. Hector, the floor is gone. It's the universe. Can you see it? I'm going in.'

Hector stood guardlike beside the young lass and watched. His heart lurched in his chest at first, knowing that Joan had asked that they not return to the Halls without her. He could not see what the young seer was looking at, the floor solid under their feet, but he could see that something was happening to Lucy. Hector spoke not a word.

'Yes. Join the dance. The dance,' Lucy spoke to the oval.

And she was gone. Gone.

'Goodgraciousgoddess. Please bring her back. I beg you. Ursula,' said Hector as he moved toward the nodas oval. In the hundreds of years that he had travelled to the Halls, Hector had never seen anything like that. The dancing lights came out of the oval, caressed the young girl and stole her away. He touched the stone. Smooth and cold. He had never touched an oval before. He moved his hands across the lights, nothing. Solid rock. Hector started to panic. *What would Joan say?* He peeked behind the oval, nothing. How long had she been gone? Was it 10 seconds? A minute? Time had lost all meaning. Hector glanced at the oval to the right and saw a rock band playing a concert at an outdoor stadium. The shot zoomed in on the lead singer. *It's Royal Hickey. What are the chances? No such thing as coincidence. What song is that? Concentrate on the song, the words will come. Songs are usually three or four minutes. I'll wait to panic.*

> *I'm reaching for the door*
> *It's been so long*
> *Just one more step to go*
> *And I'm coming home*
> *Reflections always show a stranger in the glass*
> *Nothing but a blur whenever I look back*
> *The clouds are moving on and the days are growing long*
> *My mind is so much clearer and I am getting strong*
> *Mama, I am coming home*

That's the song. Coming Home. She's coming back. Ah. Thank you, thank you, thank you.

Hector settled down and listened to Royal sing. He was great. The Queen always said she liked his voice. Hector hadn't paid much attention to rock music. He was into Mozart and Beethoven, the emotional grab. Royal was a big bundle of emotion there.

Just as Royal finished off the song, Hector saw the lights emanate out of the stone and gently place Lucy back right where she had been.

'Wow, Hector. I LOVE this place! I have to get back home, fast. I want to write down everything. Hurry, Hector.'

'You gave me a start, young lassy. You don't know how glad I am to see you,' said Hector as he hugged the excited young girl and they popped back to her living room. She hit the floor running and was bounding up the stairs in no time.

'Hector, sorry, but I have to get my pad and paper. Excuse me, thanks SO much.'

'But Lucy, I want to hear…'

Hector gave up, seeing it was useless. She was determined to write down the memory immediately. *I'm sure she'll be sharing her sharings when she's done.* But Hector wasn't all that sure. Traditionally, the shaman of the village or the seers of renown would keep their visions to themselves. When they did share, it was out of a commitment to give beings a chance with free will to change their fated

158

destiny. Sometimes folks paid attention and tried to change some of the bad stuff.

'Help yourself... whatever,' Lucy yelled politely and abstractly from her bedroom.

With no one under his charge any longer, Hector glanced out the bay window and saw the Hickey boys riding their new bikes down by the lake. *What are they up to? That Tom has a head on his shoulders. Surely they won't get too close to the edge.*

The lakeshore had been spruced up a few years back by the Downtown Business Group. Since the premiere park was on the west side of the lake, they wanted out of town visitors to have a grand impression of their city. A major fundraiser had taken place and they hired an award winning landscape architect to redesign the foliage and flowers along the shoreline. The fellow had outdone himself. Even Hector was impressed and thought he couldn't have done a much better job.

They brought in tons of white sand to one of the beach areas, making it the favourite swimming spot for tourists all summer long. You could be swimming one minute and around the corner awaited a vibrant downtown for all your shopping pleasures. The flowers were glorious all summer long. The city workers were meticulous in keeping up with the original designs and took care of all garbage issues. Across the street from the Hickey residence, the

159

shoreline had been buoyed up with a stellar rock formation and a park setting of juniper and yew trees interspersed with quaint flower gardens. A gardener's dream. A boy's dream. *Thor must think Tom and Angus are in the house. He never would let them ride their bikes there. And where are the guardian gnomes anyway?* When Mary and Joan had decided to have a spa afternoon, everyone was happy. Hector just happened to be visiting when Joan announced their plans to Lucy, and he'd graciously offered to stay with Lucy and house sit. *I'd wanted a little time alone to talk to Lucy, not be watching those rascals while she's writing! I wonder where she was... Oh, no.*

'Lucy, I'm taking a wee walk to the lake, yell if you need me,' Hector called as he headed for the front door.

Snelton! Hector calling Snelton, come in now please. Hector couldn't see Thor with the younger boys, and he knew Snelton was Thor's guardian gnome, but he intuitively knew that Snelton had a handle on this situation. He'd walked a few steps towards the front gate before Snelton came in, loud and clear.

'Hey, boss. What is up?'

'Snelton! What have I told you about that kind of talk?'

'Oops. Sorry, Boss. I've been hanging around with Thor for so long, it's rubbing off.'

160

'You'd better get him off that mode, too, Snelton. Now, where are you and why are young Angus and Tom alone at the lake?'

'Well, what's up is this: Angus and Tom are playing hide and seek... did you say 'lake'?

'Yes, Snelton.'

'Oh, those boys. Over and out, Boss.'

'Snelton.'

He was gone before Hector could ask about the other guardian gnomes. Odd. He continued to walk toward the lake to investigate. Out of the corner of his eye, he saw Snelton scurrying down the Hickey laneway and then reappear at the water's edge. I'll have to talk to Snelton about missing sequences, I see.

'Angus! Tom! Get back to the house immediately. You know the rules about bikes near the lake. Remember what happened to Ruby.'

Hector had heard about the Ruby water incident and remembered the lady who had alerted the Hickey's just in time. He glanced down a few houses, and sure enough, there she was again, watching like a hawk.

I wonder what she's thinking about Snelton and me. Ha. It's been several days now and not one of the neighbors has phoned Mary or Joan about their newfound friends. Ignorance is bliss, to them. Ha.

161

Hector was close enough to converse with Snelton and they were hidden from her view when he entered the first garden formation.

'Did ye see Mrs. Cravitz out on her deck, Snelton?' asked Hector.

'Aye, I did,' said Snelton.

'We nary need another Ruby incident.'

'Aye, I know,' said Snelton.

'Boys. If ye don't have ye bikes in the garage before I count to three, ye'll be wishing ye had a Wishin' Well, if ye know what I mean,' said Hector.

'Hector, don't get mad,' started Angus.

'TWO,' shouted Hector and the boys and bikes were flying across the road toward the garage.

'Now, Snelton, we'll talk later. I'm busy as a bee with Lucy,' said Hector.

'Oh, I've been trying to tell you; she just jumped on her bike and started riding like the wind,' Snelton said.

'WHAT!?' Hector looked around in every direction, but there was no Lucy to be seen. 'Which way did she go?'

'Down there, Boss. Towards downtown,' said Snelton.

He flashed out and had navigated the corner before Snelton could blink.

Chapter 10

The Seven Ls Message

'Where are you off to, wee Lucy?' shouted Hector.

Anyone looking would've seen a nine-year-old girl riding fast down toward the main street in Lakeville, maybe a little greenish haze accompanying her. The haze, being unexplainable, would've been dismissed in their mind as not there. It was Hector.

'Oh, hi Hector,' Lucy said glancing over at him. 'I'm going to the craft shop to get this cool book I saw there.'

'And you didn't think I might object?'

Lucy came to a full stop in front of a row of townhouses and looked at Hector.

'Well, Goddo, always let me go without asking.'

Hector put his hands on his hips and shot right back:

'You very well know that I told your Ma that I'd be watching ye today. And ye know that Goddo is with The Queen for the entire week. What is up with ye wee ones today?'

'Sorry, Hector. I'm so used to Goddo. He knows I'm safe and I know it, too.'

'I'll be letting ye go then and I'll be talking to Goddo, too.'

The girl and the gnome were so involved in their discussion that they didn't notice the young boy on the porch of one of the townhouses until he stood up.

'Is he some kind of robot doll?' asked the boy.

'Ha. Do I look like a doll now?' said Hector as he stretched to a tall six feet.

'Hector! Don't worry, I'm coming right back home.'

With a look of disdain, Hector vanished.

'Cool,' said the boy. 'Where'd you get it?'

Lucy took a good look at the boy. She knew most of the kids in the neighbourhood and he looked about her age.

'Who are you?'

'I'm John. My Grandma lives here. Who are you?'

'Lucy. I live down on the lake.'

'How'd you make it disappear?'

'Oh that. It's easy. I'll show you sometime. Gotta go, see ya.'

As Lucy started off on the bike again, John called after her,

'Hey! Lucy! Come back!'

She stopped and looked back.

'I'm really in a hurry today. Are you still here visiting tomorrow?'

'Ya. I'm staying with Grandma until September, but I don't know any kids around here.'

'Oh. I'll bring some of my guy friends over to meet you tomorrow, ok?'

'OK! Thanks. Maybe we can go for a bike ride around the lake.'

'OK, bye again.'

Lucy soon forgot about John and Hector. She turned the corner and saw the craft store. *I hope they still have it. It'll be perfect for props… How do you say that word again? Propsees. Whatever. It'll be perfect for writing down stuff I learn in the Halls. There it is. It's here! Yippee.*

Lucy was a regular at the store with her Ma. They both enjoyed being creative and had made craft time a normal part of their routine. The owner was helping another client at the till, but smiled at Lucy. She had one employee, but was working by herself when Lucy walked in. Lucy had to wait. *I wonder if Mrs. Hennessey would mind if I got the book out of the window. She might want to do it herself.*

'Lucy, you go right ahead and get that book. I'll be done here in a minute.'

Lucy turned and looked at Mrs. Hennessey. She was getting change for the customer. *Did she say that? No.*

'Yes, Lucy. Go ahead and get it.'

Ah, thanks Mrs. Hennessey.

You're quite welcome.

'There you go, Mrs. Duggan. Enjoy your knitting. I'm sure Chelcie will love the colors,' said Mrs. Hennessey as she handed the bag and the change to her.

"Thanks so much Mrs. Hennessey, I'm sure you're right! See you soon," said the customer as she left the store.

"Hello, Lucy. I see you've come back for the book," said Mrs. Hennessey as she walked toward her.

With no one else in the store, Lucy looked directly at Mrs. Hennessey and said, 'Why didn't you tell me you could talk like that before?'

'I guess it never came up. I don't like to intrude," said Mrs. Hennessey. 'Today, though, I see you're in a fluster and want to get that book right back home. If you don't mind my nosiness, what is the project?'

'Cool. Ah. Today. Yes, I have to hurry. I'll tell you about it all another day, OK? I remember you said it was twenty dollars with tax included, so I brought this twenty-dollar bill from my piggy bank. I don't need a receipt, OK?' Lucy said as she hoisted the book out of the front window display case.

'OK, Lucy. You run along now and enjoy. Say hi to your Mom for me,' Mrs. Hennessey smiled as she let the eager girl out of her store.

Wow. Mrs. Hennessey's a witch, too. This life is so cool. I can't wait to write down the seven L's.

Lucy was lost in thought for the ride home and didn't think to look for John at the townhouses until she was riding up her laneway. Oh ya. The new kid. He's cute. He'll love Angus and Tom.

Hector was on the porch before she put the bike in the garage.

'I didn't think ye'd be so long, lassy.'

'I met a witch and had to chat,' said Lucy.

'Faith and begorrah. Didn't I tell you to come straight home? Where were ye that ye met a witch for goodnessgoddesssakes?'

'It's the lady who owns the craft store, Hector. Mrs. Hennessey. Today she talked just like you and me do. That means she's a witch, too, right?'

'Ah. Did I say I was a witch, lassy? I've much to teach you before you get out of my sight again. What, pray tell, has Goddo been up to?'

'He's been...'

'Oh, hello Lucy. Excuse me for interrupting. And hello to you, too, ah...' said Mrs. Cravitz as she walked up their path.

Lucy and Hector had made it into the front entry of the Kelly's home, but were so engaged in their conversation that they hadn't shut the door, let alone noticed Mrs. Cravitz walking up the street.

'Mrs. Cravitz. Oh, sorry, this is my Uncle Hector,' said Lucy.

'Oh, how do, Mr. Hector?' said Mrs. Cravitz leaning over and smiling.

'I'm just home from the craft store, Mrs. Cravitz, and must excuse myself to go to the bathroom. I'm sure Uncle Hector can help you. Mom is out right now. Do you need something?' said Lucy as she walked backwards, package under her arm, toward the stairs.

'Oh no, just dropping by to make sure your Mom knows we need to have her guest list in for the annual street barbeque on Saturday. I've got to get the name tags done,' said Mrs. Cravitz.

'Thanks so much, Mrs. Cravitz; I'll be sure to tell her and see you later alligator," said Lucy, who then turned and ran full tilt up the stairs.

'Well, then, Mr. Hector, will you still be here…'

Her voice faded as Lucy turned the corner to her room, smiling. Normally, she'd love to hear that conversation, but it was quickly forgotten when she saw the *Spell Book* on her bed. She'd brought it in from her Mom's room when she was trying to spell the prophecy word. It was then that she decided she wanted a special book to write down her diary of the 'Halls'.

The world was gone again when she opened her new diary and began:

Prophecy by Granddaughter Lucy

She wasn't sure how to spell granddaughter and thought she'd leave it with one 'd'. Then she scratched it out. *Ah. I want this book to be perfect. I think I'll do practice pages and then write it out in good later. Good thing these pages are the add in kind.*

Prophecy by Lucy

That sounds OK.

#1 The L List from the Halls

Seven Ls foretell the plan

Seven Ls to befall man

Earthlings know, when blights arrive,

That it's never too late to learn to survive

Memorize the L List now

It will bode all very well

For when times have changed

And light is here

Ye will look back with no fear

The L List will be your guiding force

Ahead, behind, with no remorse

All will be resolved and then

The Golden Age returns to Earth

Thanks to Mother Nature

She again gives birth…
Rewind and play again
The Celts say tis Luck
The Whiteman covets Land
The Black man holds to Laughter
The Yellow Race looks for Letters
The Red Race for Life
Humankind shining Light
Beings of Love
Game Done

What does it mean? Maybe I'll understand when I'm a teenager. Cool.

Content that she got every word right and written, Lucy went downstairs to see how Hector was faring. She knew Mrs. Cravitz wouldn't leave. Everyone in the neighborhood, kids included, knew that she was the street gossip. If you wanted everyone to know something, you need only tell Mrs. Cravitz. No one minded, though, because she was harmless. She didn't have a mean bone in her body and she was always saying 'thank you, thank you, thank you'. Her late husband, Frank, had worked for the McConkey Milk Company since his early teens and had been her early introduction to local gossip. She and Frank had married the day after high school graduation and were married for 58 wonderful years before he dropped dead shoveling the driveway over two years ago. He had a snow blower, but he

preferred the steel edged shovel. Since retirement, Frank had
been fanatic about keeping his lawn weed free in the summer
and his walks and driveway clear in the winter. Mrs. Cravitz
would point out that his back never bothered him, not after
bending his body in half while handpicking weeds for hours
at a time for days on end and not after scraping snow and ice
off of the hard packed driveway or the icy walkway. Frank
Cravitz was in such good shape for a man of 76 that the
entire community was shocked at his passing. He led a good
life, a great life, but he didn't get the golden years he
deserved. The coroner had said that it was an embolism and it
was like a ticking bomb, could've blown anytime in his life,
so folks were happy that he had a good kick at the old can.
Mrs. Cravitz liked to compare his death to his horse that had
died near his death scene, only back in the late sixties.

'Yes, Hector, it was the last horse to have a milk run
in this city. The neighbour kids were so traumatized seeing
the horse drop dead in front of their house that the city
decided to go fully with trucks for milk delivery. Frank was
so disappointed about the trucks. And heartbroken about that
horse; he loved Patches so. And here, he ended up passing in
almost the same spot as his beloved horse,' said Mrs. Cravitz.

'Ah, the industrialization of a nation,' said Hector.

'The downfall, I'd say,' said Mrs. Cravitz. 'The
milkman used to keep people up on other people. And then
the horses would bring out the best in people, kids and adults

171

alike. With the truck, the company concentrated on the profits. Profits at any cost. Yes, sir. The decline of civilization as we know it started right here with the milk truck, Mr. Hector.'

'I didn't know you had a horse named Patches, Mrs. Cravitz,' said Lucy.

'Oh, that was a long time ago, dear. Well, I best be leaving you two to your business, I've tallied long enough. I must get over to the Wilson's house to collect their name list for the barbecue.'

'Would ye be needing any help with ye barbecue, Mrs. Cravitz?' said Hector.

'Why, Mr. Hector. How very kind of you to offer. Everyone works so hard at it and it's fabulous. I'm sure you'll be a big help for everyone if you can stay around for the festivities. We have grand fireworks at dark.'

'I wouldn't miss it for the world, Mrs. Cravitz.'

Chapter 11

Past, Present and Future

Meet

'Angus and Thor. Get in here immediately.'

There was tension in Mary Hickey's voice and the boys looked at each other uncomfortably.

'Guess we'd better get in there, eh Angus? You first, little bro,' said Thor.

'Ah, coming, Mom,' said Angus.

Mary stood with her arms crossed, her stance rigid. She was trying to remember the four-step relaxation method she'd heard about from Joan. *What was it?* Oh ya. Breathe. There. Then what?

'Thor Hickey. Angus. NOW. Where is Tom?' *Oh. Shine the heart light and then forgive self. Does that mean forgive me for all this motherhood stuff? OH, and the fourth one is gratitude.*

'Yes, Mom?'

'Don't you look so innocent to me. Ruby told me about you two. I can't even go to get a massage without something happening? Christ. I mean Yesu Criste. All the great relaxing feeling I had is gone, poof, gone!'

173

'Mom, that's only because you *choose* for that nice feeling to be gone.'

Oh ya, I'm supposed to forgive them after I forgive me...

'Don't pull that on me, Angus. I can pull it on you, but don't you DARE pull it on me,' said Mary, starting to lighten up.

Oh, gratitude. Thank you God for their health. Where's Tom?

'Mom. It's past. Lettuce live for the now, like God gave us a present, so we call it the present. So. So, like lettuce enjoy the present and have a salad. It'll be all wilty by tomorrow.'

Thor and Mary started with a giggle and both were laughing hysterically watching Angus use the middle stairs as a pulpit for Mary's Golden Age professions.

'What's going on here?'

'Dad!'

'Ain't no t'other,' said Royal as he and Ruby walked in from the sunroom.

'Ruby came and got me. Said something happened to Tom,' said Royal.

'Oh, Dad. He'll be fine. Snelton's gone to get him,' said Angus.

'He is not fine. And Mom told you that you couldn't play around with the Wishing Well when she was gone today,' said Ruby.

'Didn't.'

'Did so.'

'Didn't.'

'I saw you! I was coming in from the kitchen and I heard you and Tom fighting.'

'What happened? Tom? Omigod. Is he OK? Was he at the lake, too?' said Mary.

'No, no, Mom. We were playing ping pong in the back yard and Snelton and the boys came to watch and…'

'Where is Snelton? Snelton! Where is Tom? Somebody tell me where Tom is right now,' said an increasingly alarmed Mary.

'Well, after we got back from the lake, we were in the backyard, just playing around.

'Yes, yes. I understand, Angus, but I mean right now. Ruby only told me about you boys riding bikes on the rock platforms beside the lake. Why didn't you tell me about Tom? And what happened? What?' said Mary.

'Oh, I tried to tell you, Mom, but you started off to get the boys before I could finish. The lake incident was really nothing,' said Ruby.

'Nothing! Please, where is Tom?'

'Mom, he's OK. He just freaked when he saw the Little People grow big,' said Thor.

'What do you mean 'freaked'?'

'Well, he, ah, he tried to grab two of the gnomes, so him and Angus started fighting and Angus dragged him into the Wishing Well,' said Thor.

'The Wishing Well? They grew?'

'Ah, ya. Big, Ma.'

'Thor, where is Hector?' said Royal.

'Ah, I'm not sure, Dad, we were just going to go to and check on Snelton and Tom in the dungeon. Seriously, we were just going to get him when we saw Mom's car pull in,' said Thor.

'Dungeon? Oh, Christ. The Queen's castle. That's what Hector said. I remember now. What did he say, Mary?' said Royal.

'I know. I know,' said Angus. 'He said that no one has been down there in hundreds of years, so let's go. Maybe there'll be buried treasure there.'

'Or maybe there'll be spiders and snakes,' said Thor.

'Or Tom. Or traps,' said Dad. 'Get Hector here, now. Let's get to the Well fast,' said Royal.

As they ran toward the sunroom, Snelton appeared, wringing his hands.

'I've heard stories about the dungeons, but I'm thinking that they're not so bad,' he said.

'I'm thinking I want to see Hector right now,' said Royal as he put one foot in the Wishing Well.

'Hector at your service. Oh hi, Royal. What's going on...' said Hector as he appeared in lightning speed.

Everyone started talking at once and Hector held up his hands.

'Got it,' he said as he turned to Snelton. 'I'll deal with you later. Everyone wait right here.'

'Wait,' Royal started to say as Hector disappeared. 'Mary. I think I should join Hector. Tom may be too scared to go with him. What do you think?'

'Dad, I want to go with you,' Angus said.

'No, Angus. No one's going. You're right, Royal, but...' said Mary.

They didn't have long to argue, because Hector and Tom appeared before Mary could finish her sentence.

Despite his dusty appearance and the cobwebs hanging off of him, Tom looked happy.

'THAT was so cool. What is this all about? Where was that? Who was that little faery girl?' said Tom.

'You saw Trinity?' said the obviously astounded Hector.

'She said her name was Trini. Oh, maybe she said Trinity. She showed me tricks and wow. She's a real faery guys,' said Tom.

'We were looking for her, Hector. We wanted to ask her to follow him into the dungeons, because she's so brave,' said Snelton.

'I want to meet a faery,' said Ruby. 'Please, Hector?'

Everyone joined in, and it took a few minutes for Hector to quieten everyone.

'Tut. Tut. The Castle deep is off limits, everybody. And Snelton knows The King's Rule. Where are those other troublemakers?'

'Ah, here we are, Boss,' said Granno, Jumper standing at his side near the doorway.

'And Trinity?'

'Aye, Hector,' Trinity peeked from around the corner in the living room.

'Do you know what the King would do if he found out about your recent excursions, folks? Well, it wouldn't be pretty. He's hyper protective of his home, considering the recent Formorian sitings in the vicinity,' said Hector. 'I am almost inclined to take the Wishing Well away for a period.'

Groans were heard all around. Poof. It was gone.

'That's great Hector. How do I explain my absence from my rehearsal this evening? Oh, the Hector took away

178

my Wishing Well, so I had to catch a jet back from Canada?' said Royal.

'What are Formorans?' said Mary.

'I'll get you back, Royal; don't you worry. I was busy going over the sightings with Scotland Yard; can't be too careful with the dark forces these days. Formorians, Mary. Since time out of mind, they've been the fight. Main reason we had to go underground back when. We've been rebuilding for centuries, though, and are about to announce our involvement in the growing love meme on our Blue Planet.'

'Why did you have to get me so fast, Hector? I was just going to ask Trinity if I could fly on a dragon?' said Tom.

'Tom! We were so worried about you. We didn't know what was in the dungeon and maybe those dragons you like so much would kill you. Maybe Hector's not the nice gnome we think he is. We think the little people are sincere and OK and that they want to be friends, but maybe they're some alien race setting us up,' said Ruby. 'Really, Mom and Dad. I mean, I really like the Queen and King, but who knows?'

'Exactly why I want you to talk to Lucy and Joan, folks,' said Hector. 'Some people are starting to remember about the past, in a sense. Once you hear the stories, the truth will resonate for some and for others, full memory will return.'

'Are you saying Joan knows more about all this than we do?' asked Mary.

'She does. Her bloodline comes from the time before. We'll get together with them later tonight. All of us. Maybe you can see if Victor's family can come, too. It's time,' said Hector.

'I think you'd better invite John McDonnell, too, Hector,' said Lucy from the doorway where she stood beside Trinity the Faery.

'Goodnessgraciousgoddess. Announce yersElf, lassy,' said Hector. 'And who be John McDonnell?'

'I believe he's the descendant of an old friend of yours, Hector. He's now a new neighbour down the street, staying with his Grandma for the summer. You know, the one you grew to six feet for? The kid my age? I had a moment where I saw you and his ancestral Grandpa Kaq,' said Lucy.

'Kaq,' said Hector. His face turned white. 'I must see him now. Take me to him, Lucy.'

'OK, but I told him I was bringing Angus and Tom over to meet him tomorrow.'

'Can we come, too, Hector?' asked Tom.

'Who is Kaq?' said Royal.

'How about you enjoy this feast,' Hector said pointing to the dining room table. 'Royal, I'll be back before

180

you need me. Kids, ask Trinity to tell you a story about Granno, Jumper, Snelton and the Formorians. She's had to save their bee-huts more than once, I tell ye.'

As everyone turned to the dining room, Lucy and Hector went out the front door.

It was the gloaming; Hector's favourite time of day. He had been enjoying watching the sunset when Royal had summoned him. *Ah, the lake is like a mirror. The calmness belies all.*

'Do you want to walk, Hector? It's so nice out right now,' said Lucy aloud and then silently, '*Or can you just zap us over there?*'

'Lucy, Lucy. Walking is the best form of exercise,' said Hector as they rounded the overgrown juniper tree on her front lawn and disappeared from view.

'*Yes, I can, I shall and I must 'zap us' as you say; ah, here we are. Which house is Kaq's*?' said Hector as the unlikely duo walked up Patterson Street.

'That is so cool, Hector. Hope Mrs. Cravitz saw us. Look, there's John,' said Lucy.

'Hey, Lucy,' said John.

'Hey, John,' said Lucy.

'John, I've come to apologize about frightening you earlier today. Will ye accept a heartfelt apology?' said Hector.

'Well, you don't have to apologize. I thought it was cool. You didn't scare me," said John.

'Ye didn't think I was scary? Ye must be related to my good friend Kaq; he was the bravest I've ever known. And for me, I am Ambassador Hector Grodstooth of the P.L.A.C.E., but ye can call me Hector.'

'Hmm. That sounds like something familiar to me. Did I read about you somewhere?'

'Not yet, my friend. We've come to ask your family over for a visit,' said Hector.

'Well, Grandma's at work right now, but she should be home soon. Did you mean tonight?' said John.

'At your earliest possible convenience, John. Would ye be having plans tonight?'

'I don't think so. I'll ask Grandma when she gets home. I think I just saw her car go in the back lane now. Hold on,' said John as he ran into the house.

'Did ye see that, young lassy?' said Hector, beaming.

'What, Hector? Does he remind you of your friend? I don't understand.' said Lucy.

'As sure as there's water in Lakeville, I'm sure. He's a fine young lad, that one, Lucy. He comes from a long line of spiritual warriors. The best.'

'Do you mean like ghost fighters?'

'No, no. Ah, lassy. He's a GodGoddess fighter. Fights for the light side. That's how I'd say it in that language ye be speaking,' said Hector.

'Who's a GodGoddess fighter?' said John.

'We were just talking, John,' both Hector and Lucy unsure if they had been speaking aloud or inside.

'Hmm. Well, Grandma's home. She said to come inside, she's just hanging up her sweater,' said John.

John held the door open to the middle townhouse, number 1575 Patterson. Lucy added the numbers in her head to the single digit nine. *Cool, the healing house.* The homes were red brick with green and white painted trims. John's porch was quite wide and cozy. Lucy hadn't noticed the comfortable patio set until John held the door. The plush cushions were an orange floral pattern on a deep forest green background. She saw the faery knick-knacks and candles and smiled. *I'm going to like John's Grandma!* Hector was leading the way and when she stepped through the threshold, she felt as if she'd entered one of his transformed worlds. *Wow. Was I right!*

The home was an open concept, but his Grandma had painted and decorated different areas so you felt like you were looking at a painting and flowing with it at the same time. Lucy noticed the arched window at the back, dark against the gloaming. She saw underneath the sheer green tinted drapes that the trim was painted gold and that dozens of crystals were hanging across the breath. On each corner of the window, which ran the length of her living room, she'd hung huge pots of ivy that swirled around an oak curtain pole and down toward the floor at the sides. Atop the window was a golden angel, singing and watching all. A bench seat in front of the windowsill matched the warm biscuit paint of the one side of the room, but the other wall attracted Lucy's eyes. The paintings were placed below eye level on the teal wall. Spectacular. One was a ship out of the 1500s on a teal ocean wave. Another was a black woman with haunting eyes and a golden headdress on a teal background, looking regal and strong. Lucy's favourite was a peacock, resplendent with teal flecked feathers blending into the room. Teal, teal, teal.

Hector's eyes had stopped at the table in the centre of the room. Lucy noticed and looked down and gasped. It was her healing wand. *It can't be.*

'Well, hello, friends of my favourite John. Any friends of John's are friends of mine,' said the towering lady that smiled into the room. 'Ah, I see you've noticed my healing wand.'

'Good evening to ye, Grandmother to John; I'd be Hector Grodstooth at your service.'

'And I'm his, ah, niece, Lucy, from down the street.

John's Grandma reached over to hug Lucy first and said, 'I like hugs, because if you give a hug, you get a hug!

Nice to meet you, Lucy Fromdownthestreet. And you, Hector Grodstootheatyourservice.'

Standing up to her full six foot height, she announced, "And I am Mickey McDonnell, Grandmother of John, ready, willing and able to assist in bringing heaven to earth.'

'Grandma, you're funny. I think they already know that from looking around your house,' said John.

'Well, please do come into the kitchen and we'll brew a cup of tea while I make dinner. You're welcome to stay. Do you like vegetable stew on a bed of rice? I've already made the stew, just take a few minutes to get the rice going.'

'Very kind of you to offer, Mickey. Do ye mind if I call you Mickey?'

'Please do. Do ye mind if I call ye Hector?'

'Please do. And we'd love to stay for tea, but we must be getting home to Lucy's Mother soon. She didn't know that we were going for a wee visit,' Hector said as he jumped up onto one of Mickey's barstool chairs at the kitchen island. The chairs were floral like the patio set, only golden and deep blue greens. The kitchen was a continuation of the living area, both the colours and the themes. A gnarly gnome, carved high up in a birch tree and shellacked, oversaw all from his corner roost. He smiled up at the corners, mischievous and all knowing at the same time. Hector vaguely thought that the wooden statue looked like his cousin Jojo.

Mickey had her back to the guests, busy making the tea, as she asked: 'What interest have you in my healing wand?'

'Ah, tis the familiarity that attracted our gaze, Mickey,' said Hector.

She turned to face him and stared hard into Hector's eyes.

'I've never seen one like it, Hector, and I've seen many. How in the world could it seem familiar to you?'

'Lucy has found its match, Naki, I mean Mickey,' said Hector.

'Naki? Match?'

'What he means, Mrs. McDonnell, is that I found one that looks like yours,' said Lucy.

'I say what I mean, and I mean what I say. I said 'the match', Mickey.'

'No, you said, 'it's match, Naki, I mean, Mickey,' said the glaring Mickey.

'Ye caught me red-handed, Mickey. I'd like to be talking to ye about all of this when we are alone, first, I think, seeing we have the wee ones interested. How about that? Would it be okay with ye if the wee lad and wee lass went onto the cozy wee porch to have their cup 'o tea?'

'As our French so eloquently put it, Hector, I must say, 'Oui',' agreed Mickey.

186

The visible relief on Hector's face was hard to miss. 'I don't mind, Hector, but John will be okay to hear what you want to talk about,' Lucy directed at Hector.

'I know, lassy, but I'd like a moment with Mickey first, okay?'

'Run along, kiddies; we'll bring out the tea,' said Hector.

'And is that the famous 'we' or 'ye', Hector?' said Mickey.

Lucy had already started down the hall to the front door and turned to smile at Mickey. *This is getting interesting.*

When he saw that the kids were out of earshot, Hector turned to Mickey.

'How much do you remember?' said Hector.

'Well, it seems lately that more and more is coming clearer faster and faster. When you called me Naki, I felt as if I could almost touch something. What is it, Hector?'

'I've known your people from the other side of time, Mickey. You must know them. Your ancestors were my friends. Kaq and Naki.'

'Kaqtukwow.'

'You remember.'

'Just the name. What else can you tell me?'

'Mickey, I can share everything I know. It is time. My King and Queen have appointed me the Ambassador in charge of the Rekindlement. I represent the Little People who left the world of form hundreds of years ago, around the same time I first met your people.'

'It's John, isn't it?'

'Yes. He's involved. How much have you told him?'

'Told him? He's just arrived. He's had a crushing blow to deal with. His father died last month and now my daughter has left for Singapore for business. It has been a difficult time for her and I talked her into going. I told her John could use some Grandma love to heal. We've always been close and he wanted to come.'

'No doubt. As for John, I'm sure Lucy will be catching him up a little,' smiled Hector.

'And what is this matching wand you spoke of?'

'Ursula Shipton made it. How did you come to find it?'

'Ursula. Hmm. I always say that it found me,' said Mickey. 'I was out at the Jacob's Art Gallery at Sol Lake and spied the amethyst in one of their jewellery cases. When I bent down to look at it, I gasped at the beauty of the wand. I had to have it. It was funny. Nan that works there knows me, and she said it had just come in from a dealer from the East. They didn't know the value of it, so they gave me a great deal.'

'There are only the two. Ursula made one for Naki and one for herself. She had a fine eye for healing stones and

188

crystals. The two are practically a match. When you see Lucy's, you'll see that her amethyst is quite a bit lighter than yours, and the crystal wand is actually about three inches longer.'

'Who was Ursula, Hector?'

'She was a prophet and healer in the 1500s. Only came to Turtle Island one time, landing on the homeland of your people. She made the wands to help out with the devastation of the peoples and she stayed for the duration of the decimation. It was the worst of times, Naki. Mickey. Ursula helped as much as anyone could. She was a blessing.'

'Lucy's bloodline.'

'That's it, folks. And the new generation is here. It is our task to help in the healing of the bloodlines. Mother Earth has made it clear that there is to be no waiting for the next in line. We must take up the cause.'

'Who are your Queen and King? What is a rekindlement?'

'Aye. King Oberon and Queen Titiana of the Little People. They want to rekindle the friendship with Earthlings.'

'Ah. Everything is becoming clearer. I've had some visions and dreams about this, Hector.'

A loud crash reverberated through the kitchen. *What was that?* Lucy was screaming. Hector and Mickey looked at each other and ran toward the front porch. Mickey was first in line and could see it wasn't good. A car had somehow ended up on the sidewalk, it's front end smashed through Mickey's porch spindles. John lay motionless and facedown in the corner of the porch, a pool of blood growing around him. Lucy had stopped screaming and knelt beside John. She looked up at Mickey, eyes begging her to help him.

'Phone an ambulance,' someone yelled. It was the driver getting out of what was left of the front seat. 'Oh, my God. Is he OK? That lady ran the red. I didn't see her coming. Is she OK?'

'Hector. Get the wand, please,' said Mickey as she dropped to her knees. Hector had turned before Mickey spoke. In a flash, he had returned and held it beside her so she could take it.

'It's a head injury. He'll be okay. No damage to the neck or brainstem,' said Mickey. 'God, kindly send yOur healing light and energy through my boy; I ask, I pray. Take over! Thank you for the gift of John. Thank you for his life, his health.' As she whispered pleadings, Mickey held the wand near the head wound and washed her hand back and forth over his body. The neighbours had come to help and had turned on their porch lights. Though Mickey's porch was darkened, a soft glow emanated from around John and Mickey. Some of the crowd may have thought it a trick of the gloaming lighting, but Hector and Lucy knew that it was Mickey's healing energy helping John's aura.

'Is she one of those crystal healers?' asked the driver. 'I hear the ambulance.'

Mickey took off her kerchief and used it as a tourniquet to stop the bleeding. John groaned when she tightened the material around his head.

'You're going to be just fine, baby,' said Mickey.

Lucy felt pulsing on the back of her head, just where John had been hit. She felt compelled to touch him. *Ouch.*

'O baby, you have The Gift. Ask God to protect you from his pain. Then touch,' said Mickey.

'I can see your energy. Just do it. I think there's some swelling on his brain. He needs help.'

'God help John, please,' said Lucy.

'Quickly,' said Mickey.

Hector saw that the ambulance attendants arrived and were assessing the situation.

The lady who had caused the crash was standing by her car with some concerned onlookers, holding her arm. The gentleman she had hit was beside Hector, looking at John.

'The boy on the porch,' the neighbour yelled. 'Look at him first.'

'It's working, Lucy,' said Mickey.

Lucy saw the dull glow brighten as she focussed her intention and gently placed her hand near the wound, almost touching it.

I don't even have to touch him. I just have to intend for the wound to heal. It's like I'm telling his body to get to work. Thank you, God.

Tears welled in Lucy's eyes. She knew John was going to be alright. He groaned again and his eyes opened.

'Out of the way, folks. Make room, make room,' said the attendant, parting the gathered crowd.

Mickey's eyes connected with Lucy's and they moved aside. Mickey put her arm around her and squeezed.

Chapter 12

The Deeps

'What was Hector doing in The Deeps?' roared Oberon, stomping down the hill toward his wife. The sun felt warm upon her face as she turned to see his fury, his cheeks flushed red.

That's not good.

'I was just asking myself that very question,' said Titiana as she rose and wiped her gloved hand across her forehead. The Queen had been out in the gardens, starting to ready the soil for planting. She enjoyed this time of year more than any. The seedlings were growing in her glass room and she was anxious to get them outside. She looked away from Ob and to the seed window. They were smiling. She could feel their need.

'Ob. You are red in the face. Stop it now. Look about you. Drink in the warmth and breathe in the newness of it all. Hector is ours and we his. He must have had good reason because he knows that is your one rule.

'Titiana, I know you're right, but wait,' started Oberon. He breathed deeply through his nostrils. He chest puffed up as he held in the sacred breath and he exhaled long and softly.

193

'Ah there, I cleared it. My Queenie. You're always right. How is it that you can be so calm and I am always running off steaming at the first sign of trouble?' He gently wiped a streak of dirt from Titiana's forehead with his finger. After hundreds of years, he still felt jolts and waves of love tingling his entirety when he touched his anam cara.

'Obie, Obie. You are not,' Titiana said as she put her arms around his waist. 'You usually have such control and impeccable judgment. I think it's because it was Hector that it struck you to the core. He's such a good boy. But look at you! You are even redder now than when you were angry! What is going on?'

'Oh my, Titiana. I think you'd better come to my chamber and take care of me. I feel flushed and weak at the knees.'

Titiana and Oberon fell to the ground laughing and rolling around together. It was this sight that Hector saw when he materialized near the water garden. The King and Queen sensed him before they saw him. Hector had chosen to land outside, simply because he wanted to collect his thoughts before he knocked at their door. This early in the spring, he did not expect the two to be outside, let alone rolling around on the grass.

'Hector! Twice in one day!'

194

'Hector, I think the King means that you've helped to raise his ire this morning from your excursion to The Deeps and now, from the depths of his passion! Me!' And the two rolled and laughed even more.

Hector was frozen. He knew he had broken the rule and he did not understand the levity he was seeing. He noticed some of the pixies inside the edge of the woods and some of the fairies hiding behind the waterfall.

'Oh Hector. We know you must have a good reason, so come and tell us all about it. We'll have Gladiola to make us up a fresh pot of tea and have some cinnamon cakes.'

Knowing that the Earthen linear time did not exist in the faery realm, Hector gratefully accepted. He needed a chance to bring the King and Queen up to date. Hector gathered his thoughts as he followed them along the walls of the huge stone castle. He saw the troopers, vigilant, at the gatehouse and the archers patrolling the tops of the walls. They passed the old oak tree and tramped over a wooden bridge to the gatehouse and the arched double doors. Oberon was telling Titiana that she'd best change her dress before tea, as it had been muddied in the gardens and he waved Hector and her through the open doorway.

'Onward, Hector!' said the King as he waved to the gnomes busy in the courtyard.

Hector noticed the rows of stalls and the groomers feeding the horses. The smells quickly turned to baked breads as they neared the kitchens. By the time the three were entering the Main Hall, a small entourage was following, wanting to help in some way.

'Leave us, kind folk. Tell Gladiola we'll take tea in the drawing room,' and the crowd dispersed as the King spoke. The Queen begged off to change and Hector and Oberon entered the room alone.

'Hector. Please explain what is going on,' asked the King as he drew a carved wooden box out of a drawer. He opened it and looked up at Hector.

'King Oberon. Forgive me,' started Hector.
'Please Hector. It's you and me. Give me the facts,' said King Oberon.

'Thank you, King. Hmm. I've been meaning to get over here and bring you up to date. The changes we spoke of are underway. I have been working with the Hickey family and know you made the right choice. I've had affirmations from the Halls of Fame, from incidents on ground and in my thought flashes. Many doors have opened since the decision to rekindle humankind friendship was made.'

'Yes, Hector. In particular, the door to the Deeps, I understand,' said the King as he prepared to light a cigar.

They didn't notice Mariam enter the king's drawing room with their afternoon tea. Mariam's eyes were twinkling when she announced herself:

'Ahem. Hmm. Ah. Afternoon tea anyone? I heard you say The Deeps, King.'

'Ah, Mariam. Good to see you, but is Gladiola okay?' said the King looking up at her. 'Please join us.'

'Thank you, Sir. No, Gladiola's fine; she's out with her wee ones and I asked to take her place and bring your tea.'

'Mariam, you are a doll. Do you have time to join us today? We've been talking about the Deeps only because they were infiltrated today by a certain Hector Grodstooth of the Ambassador kind. What do you think of that, Mariam? The King's Rule has been broken!'

'That Rule. Ah, I was coming to talk to you just about That Rule. Ah, I have many chores to finish up, but since you asked…' said Mariam as she sat down on the edge of the gold chaise lounge near the red marble end table. She looked uncomfortable as she continued.

'…I must tell you that Hector isn't the only one that has broken The Rule today. There's my wee brother Jack was in The Deeps, too. He's a handful for me Ma. Do you think it's because he's the youngest of nine? Ma says so. Says he had too many Das growing up with all those older boys, but she so enjoys him. Says he was hard to handle but made her laugh more than all of us put together.'

197

The Queen entered the room in a flourish of rose colors and smells. Her handmaiden had worked her magic and the Queen was radiant.

'Go on, Mariam, please,' said Titiana as Mariam stood to pour her tea and offer the cakes.

'Nothing finer than a good chuckle, eh, Titiana,' the King said remembering their roll outside. 'And that brother of yours came out laughing. Jack is funny. What's he been up to now, Mariam?'

'Well, wasn't he down in the Deeps feeding the baby dragons when Master Rungdelf himself came in. You know what the Master thinks about little boys and about The Deeps. And here Jack didn't have time to hide. Not that it would've helped anyway, because we all know that Rungdelf can smell children from miles away. I can just see Jack's eyes, round like saucers, and hear his wee voice. 'Ah, Master Rungdelf, I'm just feeding the babies.' It is hilarious to hear Jack describe what happened next. Says it was akin to a blazing fireball projectile from the Sun Herself, unexpected and earth shattering in its roar and fury. He says that the Master was at the stair bottom when the roar erupted, and then instantly had traversed the 30 meters to be right in front of Jack. Can ye imagine that scene? Poor, wee Jack. He said he fainted soon after, but not before hearing the wee dragons yelping. He said his last memory before waking in the kitchen stairwell was the smell from the Master's breath and the sound of the poor baby dragons crying.

Hector, the King and Queen had been chuckling throughout the story and when Mariam finished, they had tears rolling down their cheeks.

'Ah, Mariam. I knew we could count on ye for a laugh.'

'That Rungdelf. Couldn't ask for a better Deeps Keeper.

In his mind, the King traveled back to the time he first met Rungdelf at Merlin's castle. Merlin was known as the greatest sorcerer of his day. He instilled a fear into the hearts of brave men, but it was a fear fuelled by deep respect. One of his charges had run off to fight with the Crusaders and left a lassy with child. When the child was born, she left him at Merlin's doorstep and sailed to the new lands. After Merlin saw the child, he knew why the mother had left him behind. The child bore the mark of a healer: a red V on his forehead pointed down and around his third eye. On the day that King Oberon came to visit, Rungdelf was ornery and his wet nurse had had enough. Oberon smiled remembering the Great Merlin being taken to task by the young elf.

'When his V-mark gets so red, I know it means he needs hours of comforting, singing and loving to settle him down. I just don't have time today with the King and his men down for dinner,' she had said.

199

Merlin knew Oberon was within earshot and reprimanded the young wet nurse.

'Girl, get to the nursery. The kitchen will be fine without ye. Here, first give me the child.'

With that, the sorcerer cradled the baby and walked toward Oberon.

'This young charge will be known far and wide for his healing abilities. With his touch, he will teach the farmers to know the glories of healing themselves. It's the knowing that is important Oberon. How is it that the wee folk remember and know what the human race has long forgotten?'

Ah, the human race. Ambassador Hector rekindling that friendship. In The Land of Friendship.

His thoughts brought him back to his drawing room. Mariam was filling teacups and talking about getting the candles lit.

'Thank you, Mariam. Now go about your day. Please tell Master Jack that I'll be around for a wee visit in the next few days. Now I need privacy as I have Hector to attend to. Hector, did you see Jack or Master Rungdelf in The Deeps?'

Mariam scrambled out quickly, hoping her intervention would lessen the severity of her little brother's indiscretion. She heard the King asking Hector about Jack and she dared not listen to the answer as she shut the door behind her.

'Ah, no, Sire. Remember I was telling you about new doors opening? What I mean is that the Hickey boys had a spat and one ended up being thrown into the Wishing Well...' started Hector.

'I get the picture, Hector. I get the picture. The young lad was thrown into the Deeps. How long was he there before you got him?'

'Ah, precisely, I'm not entirely sure, but not more than a bit, Sire.'

'Did he see the dragons?'

Hector and the King bantered back and forth and Hector had to admit his ignorance. When the King called for Trinity, Hector was excited because he was as interested as the King in her story. He knew little of the dragons, and until that day had only heard rumors. When he grabbed Tom, he had seen the dragons but knew better than to think about them, let alone mention them. The King was pacing back and forth in front of the roaring fire.

'My King, at your service,' said Trinity as soon as she appeared. She looked demure in her sparkling dress and every part the faery. Her sweet disposition belied the fierce warrior that lay within. Trinity's strength of character and prowess was legend.

'Trinity. How nice to see you under any circumstance. Please tell me your tale of the boy in the Deeps today.'

'Which one?' said Trinity, not missing a beat.

The King stopped in his tracks and his eyes wide, looked at the lovely faery and then at the great gnome, Hector.

'Please tell me your whole story, Trinity,' said the King, standing still.

'Sire, first I must beg your forgiveness, as I know The King's Rule and never before have I broken it. Mine is not much of a story. I was in the back forest, behind the Queen's garden when I heard a cry for help.'

Trinity had been surprised to hear the cry. She looked at her friends and knew they had heard as well. *It's from The Deeps.* No one dared even think about The Deeps. Except Trinity. The other faeries looked at each other and knew there would be no stopping her. *It's ok, girls. I'll be right back.* Those were her last words as she disappeared.

She explained to the King that even though she was unfamiliar with The Deeps, she was able to find the boys immediately. Her acute sense of movement had landed her in a vast chamber where two young lads were surrounded by baby dragons. The room was at least 1000 yards long with one hundred foot ceilings. Even at a glance, it was obviously a training area. Torches cast an eerie light at 20-foot intervals: the room was crossed with shadow beams on the dirt floor. The height of the ceilings did little to quell the stench of animal feces, even though the room was well raked. The dragons were no bigger than three feet high, but their tails were at least 10 feet long and wagging like happy puppies. From her vantage point, Trinity introduced herself and gathered snacks for the boys to treat the wee dragons. Trinity moved the feeders upwards about 20 feet, hoping that the young dragons wouldn't jump or fly up, and then set the lads down closer to the kitchen stairwell. The boys cavorted and flew about a bit, thanks to Trinity, and threw snacks the sizes of footballs at the roaring babies. The grins on the boys were soon wiped off, as they heard the creaking of the kitchen door. In the same instant, Tom lodged himself between two beams, Trinity cloaked herself and the Dragon Keeper grabbed Jack the kitchen helper and disappeared up the stairwell. When Hector appeared on the opposite side of the room, perplexing the babies, he immediately saw and took Tom back to the Hickey living room. The timing was impeccable.

'Rungdelf was there?' said Hector.

Chapter 13

The Empress

Mary Hickey sipped her coffee on the back terrace, hardly noticing the smells of spring or the birds flitting about. She wanted to relax for the morning because the day of the annual street barbeque was always hectic. A red cardinal landed on the lilac tree, standing out starkly against the greens. *I think my birdie boyfriend knows I was up writing till the wee hours last night.* She half smiled and looked as it whistled two inquisitor calls. Mary didn't feel like whistling back. She put the pen down and watched as it soared higher and higher, and disappeared into the branches of the pine tree. *She was trying to remember her dream from the night before. There was a lane behind her house and she and her youngest son were walking down it when a large white bird, maybe a hawk, maybe a turkey vulture, she didn't know the difference, landed near them. The bird had twigs and straw in its mouth and didn't acknowledge her. Another bird landed beside her, a dark, black bird, but it looked like the same kind of bird. Her friend, Joan, appeared and said something. Joan hadn't been there moments before, but she had come to warn her. She warned her just to watch. Observe. The birds ignored them and continued about their work of making a nest.*

As the cardinal whistled it's standard two long whistles followed by a series of short, Mary broke out of her reverie and thought back to the days when she met her birdie boyfriend. When they first moved to the lake, she had made a point of enjoying the first coffee of every day in her backyard. She could feel the eyes of countless birds and animals on her as she gardened, comforting her. The yard enticed an explosion of all senses: Mary's Eden. She stood and walked toward the crab apple tree in the center of the yard. *Too much information. Too much, too soon, too fast. What had Hector said? Here's something to stretch your imagination. Hmm. SomeTHING to stretch it?! First, Tom in a castle across the ocean and then the baby dragons. And Tinkerbell for God's sake. Trinity, whatever. And an evil race. Well, Hector said they weren't evil; said they were confused and that we could help them now. Ha. And what about that young lad, John? Thank God he's okay.*

'Mary, whistle to him,' said Royal.

'Royal. What? How did you get up so early?'

'I guess you haven't noticed that your other boyfriend has been whutting and whistling for the past 10 minutes,' said Royal as he joined Mary under the tree, putting his arms around her waist.

'Sorry, Royal. I couldn't even whistle to him this morning. I got past noticing him somehow. Remember Grandma Donnelly used to say '*Whistling girls and cackling hens always come to some bad end'*...' said Mary as she did a half whistle and kissed her husband gently. 'What's going on? Every morning I wake up wondering if I'm still dreaming, but I know it's real. Are we living an adventure of mythical proportions? How can all this be real?'

'Mary, Mary. We live in a weird world. We always knew that. Remember Shakespeare? 'There is more to this world, Horatio, than you or I have ever dreamed of.'

'Wow, Royal. Quoting Willie to me now. Now I know we're all nuts! Come here and look at this poem I just wrote,' said Mary as she took Royal's hand and led him to the picnic table.

> The Empress came to visit
> To bring good cheer
> She tells of a friend
> Who is near and dear
> She lulls you to a calm
> She sweetly turns her head
> And smiles on you, she smiles
> All the while she is here
> You must pay her dear
> Pay attention to all that she says
> She's bringing you mirth
> She loves you and yours
> She's The Empress
> She's the one who cares
> She'll hold your hand

She'll stand by your man
She'll do all and all with a smile
Pay attention to her words
And in turn, turn around
Turn around and around and around
When your dance is done
Make sure you turn again
Turn again and smile and turn again
And smile for her.

'Who's the Empress? Is it the Queen?'

'I don't know. I don't know where the word Empress even came from. At first I was thinking about Queen Titiana, but it's not her. Then I was thinking about the Formorian race and wondered if they have a female leader?' said Mary.

They sat in the shaded yard for hours, talking, undisturbed by the birds or the world until the children began waking up. After breakfast, the boys wanted to go straight to Lucy Kelly's, but there was work to be done for the barbeque and they all set about their tasks.

The street barbecue began as a few neighbors pulling their barbecues out to their front lawns on the same night, mostly for the parents to have a few beers and for the kids to play in the sprinklers. After ten years of Mrs. Cravitz's organizing skills, all of Lakeville was able to enjoy the Armour Street Annual BBQ. Lakeville's premier park was on the other side of Wee Lake and more than 10,000 people came to watch the fireworks on the now famous weekend. Before dark, the citizens of Lakeville had a nice view of the stately homes that lined the opposite side of the lake, rounding the street up to the graveyard. On barbecue night, all of the neighbors set up caravan tents on their lawns. The families from the eighteen houses all participated without exception. Each year a different family would host the caterers so the food was in a central location. The caravan tents were well stacked with drinks for young and old with bartenders to serve. Rules had been agreed upon years before to keep the peace. Every household was allowed 10 guests and everyone wore nametags or hats. Mrs. Cravitz delighted in coming up with themes for the event and was in charge of guest list and security. Every year a different family was responsible for the caravan tents, caterers, serving staff and fireworks. The Armour Street Annual BBQ had become a Mardi Gras for some of Lakeville's elite.

The day before, Hector, the King and Queen had called a meeting, which included the parents and children alike. There were an ever growing number of people aware of the existence of the Little People tribe, but they were going to be introduced at the barbecue to the world at large, according to the Rekindlement Plan. Hector reminded Mary of Napoleon when he spoke of strategy and purpose. His determination to succeed was evident in not only his words, but also in his demeanor. Hector was the point person: he would handle media coverage at the event. The local papers always sent their editors, as an invitation was coveted and editors got first choice. Hector knew that the Toronto press was coming to cover the 10th anniversary celebration: *The Toronto Expositor* newspaper and the free arts and cultural magazine, *Toronto Alive* had made arrangements with Mary. NCB TV was bringing a film crew, joining the local CHAX TV. To top it all off, Hector's press plan included sending out a press release en masse hours before the event covering all details of The Plan with a picture of the King and Queen of Faery. Little did Lakeville know that the world press was about to descend on their doorstep and stay for a very long time.

'Ma, did you want me to go to the store for you?' called Angus from the front hall. 'I've finished sweeping the walk now.'

Mary was on the phone with the florist and couldn't answer. She motioned for Tom to run and tell Angus to come to the kitchen. Both Tom and Thor ran at the same time. Ruby was finishing up the breakfast dishes and looked over at her Mom smiling. Everyone was always excited on the big day. Ruby had made plans with her Mom to take the boys over to the Kelly's to play for a few hours and then to a movie, just to get them out of the way happily while last minute details were taken care of. Ruby also needed time to stretch her imagination a little more. Just that morning she told her Mom that she'd prayed to Jesus to make more room in her mind so she could understand all of this new information. Meanwhile, they'd decided that movies were an excellent escape from reality and Walt Disney never failed to deliver. Ruby's favorite line was from Disney's *Meet The Robinsons*: Keep Moving Forward. As the boys ran back into the kitchen with Angus, Mary hung up the phone and plans were forged. Hector had arrived earlier and he and Royal walked in from the back deck to see what all the commotion was about. In a few minutes, the kitchen was cleared and Mary and Royal turned to Hector.

Meanwhile, at the Kelly residence, a very different kind of day was unfolding for Lucy Kelly. Lucy had wakened at 2:20 am, drenched in sweat. The moon was full and she was bathed in a shimmering light filling her bedroom. *Must be the full moon.* It wasn't the first time she woke up that night: a couple of hours earlier she had woke with a start, but she had managed to get back to sleep. *I'll get up.* She sensed a thickness in the air that hadn't been there earlier. *Maybe it was. Maybe I was just too stunned to feel it.*

As she slid her legs to the side of the bed, she felt a twinge in her back. *Oh. I slipped on the stairs. Must have pulled a muscle.* Once her legs were over the edge of the bed, she pushed both of her hands down on the mattress to hoist

210

her body out of bed. Rubbing her back, she walked down the hall past the bathroom and stopped in front of the large picture window, drapeless, on the back wall of the house. *On a moonless night, the backyard would be pitch black. Freaky black.* Lucy liked to call the darkest black 'freaky black'. Sometimes, she'd wake up and walk to the bathroom without turning on a light, just to feel the sensation. She'd put her hands out in front of her and at her sides and not feel anything. The only real physical sensation would be the feet on the floor. That was freaky black.

Hey. What's that?

She could almost make out two figures down near the old oak tree. *It's a young boy and a girl. Or is it? Yes.*

Lucy concentrated on the image. The children seemed vague, almost. *Vague? Image? They couldn't be real.* She focused. As she focused, more details came to her. The girl's hair was dark and curly, cascading down from under a bonnet. The boy was about four foot ten, about ten years old. She was eight. *How do I know that?*

Lucy focused on the face of the young girl. *She used to live on this land.* As Lucy thought about the girl, she started to shake. She tensed her arms as she started to move away from her body. She rose from the ground. She was hovering, afraid, wanting to look away from the children, but her eyes were riveted on the girl. *I think I can fly.* She rose another half foot and hovered for a second and thought of controlling herself to land. She landed and bounced up again. The girl turned to look up at the window and in a flash, Lucy touched down to the ground and sank to the floor to hide from something that was not alive. She lay still for a minute, but it seemed to last forever. Her head rose to peek over the windowsill. *Gone. Good.*

As she stood up, she realized her back wasn't bothering her anymore. *That's one way to get rid of a pulled muscle. What was that all about? They lived on this land! They want me to find the book. Say it will explain everything. Hmm.*

She took one last look out the bay window and, seeing no figures, Lucy walked back toward the bathroom. *Man, I was hovering. I could've flown all around the house. That was real.*

Lucy bounced both feet to the floor and hopped a few steps into the bathroom. Thud. Thud. *Maybe it wasn't real. Maybe there were no kids from the past. Hmm.* She made her way back to her bed and sat on the edge of it. *Can I sleep? So many crazy things happening. Another book?* Tiredness overwhelmed her and she lay down. As she pulled the blanket up to her chin, an image intruded. It was a biscuit coloured book, at least two feet long and a foot wide. It was old. There was writing on the front cover and a lot of symbols. All in brown ink or paint. *What do those words say?* She couldn't quite make out the words. There were two silk tassels to tie it closed. And then it was gone. *Gone. Good. Hey, that's what I said when those kids disappeared. OK, OK. I'll look for the book tomorrow.*

Lucy and her mother had been living in the house on Wee Lake since her Dad had died years before. Joan Kelly had always wanted to live on the water, but never expected to live in one of the most coveted neighborhoods in Lakeville. Joan and Freddy had purchased a house in 'The Avenues' when they first learned of Joan's pregnancy, thinking they would like to raise their child in a kid friendly, lovely older home in the downtown core. While Freddy was the great breadwinner in the family, being the head of Human Resources at the university, Joan was the handyman around the house. They bought the fixer upper house at the right time, when the market was lower and before the neighborhood was known as 'The Avenues'. The neighbors loved the newlywed couple because they turned an average looking home into a real eye opener. Joan liked to brag to Freddy that the cost on her surface remodeling was next to nothing. The house was almost a hundred years old and had a verandah wide enough to hold a table and several chairs comfortably. The lead paint had been repainted over many times and took Joan several weeks of heat stripping to get off. The wood that lay under all the chipped paint was breathtaking once it soaked up buckets of a darker porch stain. Her lawn furniture was a forest green backing floral prints of fuchsias, maroons, bright yellows and oranges and shades of lighter greens. What pulled the whole look together was the small front yard. Right in front of the house were two huge sister pine trees, their lower branches jutting out just above the porch ceiling. Where there had been grass and pine needles against the house, Joan dug out around the trunks of the trees and planted flowers of every color and edged the garden with a semi-circle of flagstone rocks. To top it all off, she had found an aged set of Snow White and the Seven Dwarf figurines at a garage sale, brought them back to life with paint and planted them about her front lawn.

Lucy had fond memories of her first home, remembering her childhood as a magical and happy time. When she first heard of her great grandfather Tony's death, it reminded her of her father. Freddy's accident left Joan and her alone, just as Ursula and Zelda had been deprived of their love. She thought there might have been some kind of curse on husbands in the Shipton family and hoped it wore off before she got married. Joan couldn't bear to live in 'The Avenues' after Freddy's death and put their home on the market immediately after his death. She told everyone she was moving to 'the home of her dreams on water', not knowing where she meant but keeping her eyes open. The house sold in three days. Shell-shocked from the funeral and the sale of the house, Joan didn't know where to begin looking for their new life without Freddy. In a phone call to her insurance agent and old friend, she mentioned the quickness of the house sale.

'Where are you moving to?' he asked.

'To the home of my dreams on water,' she answered without thinking.

'Where?' he said.

'I don't know. I just know that I want to live on water,' Joan answered.

'I know where it is,' he'd said.

He proceeded to tell her of a friend who had phoned him that very morning, telling him they wanted to sell their home privately, a home on Wee Lake. Joan was excited, took the phone number and moved onto Wee Lake the following month.

Joan sat at the kitchen table, pen in hand, going over her checklist. She looked up when Lucy walked down the stairs.

'Well, it's about time Sweet Pea. You must have been tired from all your worry about your new friend. You know Johnny's going to be ok. Mickey said that he'd even be able to party with you tonight!' said Joan.

'Mom, I know John's okay. I had a bad dream and couldn't sleep.'

215

Lucy had decided to tell her Mom everything. About Ursula's diary. About the book in her dream and the ghost kids. Her list for the annual barbecue long forgotten, Joan had listened to Lucy for over an hour before they heard the voice.

'*I'm here to help*,' it said.

Their eyes met, eyebrows raised. The voice seemed to come from everywhere, surrounding them.

Ursula.

Yes. But remember, now that I've made contact, the negative will know. There will be times when you hear the voice and it won't be me. Trickster tricks. You must discern The Truth each time. Let your heart guide you. If what you hear makes you feel good, it's from GodGoddess or me; anything else is the negative. You have each other and there is strength in two. The Empress is near but not here; she is coming for you and you must be ready. I helped those children in your dream to hide the book when they lived near the lake. It was in the middle of the forest then, and much has changed. I will take you there. Are you ready?

'*The Empress?*' said Joan in her mind.

'*Yes. The Formorian world is vast and strong and there is no stronger than The Empress. She among the Land Dwellers is key. She knows of the upcoming alliance*

216

between Little People and Humankind and will stop at nothing to quash it. Her book, the one you dreamed of Lucy, explains everything. The secret code to reading it has been handed down from generation to generation, yet the meaning was long lost to time. You know the...'

The knock at the door startled the girls and the voice was gone. Lucy looked at Joan as she stood to answer the door. They shared a quick hug and opened the door to the Hickey kids. They explained that they'd left several phone messages and that they were on their way to see a movie and wanted Lucy to join them. Joan saw the message light blinking on phone, meaning she hadn't heard the ringing, yet she had been in the kitchen all morning.

'Lucy, you go to the movie and I'll get my list done. We'll meet up after to work out the book details,' said Joan.

'Mom...'

'Don't 'Mom' me; do as I say, not as I do, child!'

Lucy smiled and thought that her Mom was right; a real break from all this would be great and they could start fresh later, maybe even before the annual barbecue.

Chapter 14

The Day of the Barbecue

The phone didn't stop ringing after the noon hour. Mary
let all calls go to the answering machine, hoping nothing
too urgent would be overlooked while Hector coached her
and Royal about the news reporters. Hector had demanded
that they sit and prepare for the barrage of press to come.
He briefed them on procedure and coached them on exact
phrases to repeat for certain questions. Hector said he
couldn't stress enough the importance of the correct use of
words because of the energies attached to those words.
Mary thought he was right. For an example, he told them
to feel the word 'glorious'. He exaggerated all the
syllables and let it roll off his tongue; he said good
vibrations were attached to that word. Hector was in the
middle of his crash course in verbiage when the doorbell
rang. Mary glanced towards the front door. Hector stopped
mid sentence.

'It's ok, Mary, please answer your door. The flowers
have arrived and we've had enough of a talk for now.'

Mary had been fascinated by Hector's ideas and hoped that between the two of them that she and Royal would be able to remember all of his key points and his many interesting concepts. As she started from the room, she turned to Hector and touched his shoulder and smiled her thanks.

'You're the best!" said Mary as she hurried for the front door. She was happy to hear her husband's next words:

'Wait, Hector; I've a few questions,' said Royal as he sat down in Mary's chair.

Mary saw the shadow of a tall person through her window, didn't stop to look out her peephole, and opened the door. The deliveryman held several bouquets in his arms and more could be seen in the florist van behind him. The flowers were spectacular.

'Oh, thank you! Please follow me. I'd like to keep them cool in the kitchen refrigerator,' said Mary to the driver.

Mary had prepared space for some flowers, but saw that the bouquets were too large to fit. Hector and Royal walked into the kitchen just as Mary saw the size problem.

'Oh, dear,' said Mary.

'Mary, it's okay. If your deliveryman will bring in the rest and kindly place them on the kitchen table, I'll ready room for them in the large refrigerator at the foot of the staircase,' said Hector.

'But Hector,' started Mary, and then she finished with 'Ah, thanks.'

219

As the deliveryman left, Mary closed the door and turned toward Hector and said,

'Is everyday going to feel like a lovely Saturday afternoon from now on, Hector?'

'Well, wee Mary, there'll be your usual bumps and valleys, but generally, I think the world is on the up and up and going ever upward,' said Hector.

'We feel like we're in a too good to be true dream, Hector,'said Royal.

'Like there's a chance for peace and goodness and fun in the world,' said Mary.

'Well, it's true and it isn't because there is and there isn't,' said Hector.

'What is it, the free choice thing?' said Mary

'Mary, I have a gift for you and Royal. Maybe it will help to explain,' said Hector.

Hector pulled out two small boxes from his inside jacket pocket. The smaller box was wrapped in a pale rose pink with a tiny gold bow. A golden gift tag was attached to the bow and the embossed letters read: 'To Mary Hickey, Your Talisman'. The other box was wrapped in bold greens, reds and yellows and had no bow, but the gift tag hung from a yellow cord and read: 'To Royal Hickey, Your Talisman'. Both recipients turned their boxes over and saw the Queen of Faery's seal affixed.

'The Queen has ordered these delivered before tonight's festivities. So delivered. Please let us sit in your dining room and I'll explain,' said Hector.

The trio walked through the arched doorway and sat down.

'It's so beautiful, I don't want to open it, Hector!' said Mary.

'Truly an elaborate seal. Is that a mermaid?' said Royal.

'Questions, questions. Please open your gifts. We have much to do,' said Hector.

Mary carefully unwrapped the paper and pulled out the white box while Royal did the same. Both opened their boxes simultaneously and let out gasps of pleasure.

'Forevermore, you will enjoy the friendship of our people, Mary and Royal Hickey. Use your talisman to be builders of bridges. Build heart to heart bridges to change your reality. Remember that human hearts are pure. There are no wicked hearts, only confused people. And the soul is pure. Be aware that the mind is corruptible but the heart and soul are pure. The heart is a bridge between the mind and the soul, so you must follow your heart to your soul. All your people must become aware that the mind is both negative and positive. Whenever you ask a question the mind is automatically engaged and it will throw you the right and the wrong answer and then it's up to you to decide which is right by using your intuition. Learning to read your own mind is the greatest task of your lifetime! The easiest way is to not ask any question because then you're not getting a 'wrong' answer, but if you go by feel, feel your emotions, then you're listening to your heart and soul. When you don't ask questions, you go by intuition, which is the right way,' said Hector.

'Hector, how can we ever thank you or your people?' said Royal. 'Everything you say resonates with my heart. I am so grateful for your friendship and sharings.'

'You'll see that there is a note from the Queen in each of your boxes. She asked me to tell you it was a poem she wrote for your people.'

Mary pulled the cream paper from the bottom of the box and read aloud:

You are the seed.
You are the water that makes the seed grow.
You are the sunshine.
You are stalk that grows tall from the seed.
You are stem that blooms.
You are the flower.
The cycle, never-ending. The joy ever-present.
Look for the love in it all. Seek and ye shall find.
The love, the beauty and the art. Creation.

'Yup. That about sums it up. Except she forgot the partying part. You all have the partying Faery blood in you, too; so we must prepare for the festivities. Let me help you put on your necklaces,' said Hector to break the solemnity of the occasion.

As Mary handed him her necklace she swore she could see tinkerbell dust swirling from it as Hector took it from her hands. The solid golden pyramid was enclosed in a threaded golden sphere, the symbols remaining unexplained by the Ambassador of the Little People. While he finished attaching Royal's clasp, Hector announced:

'Before you ask another question, Hickey clan, please take time to read over the press release carefully.' He set two copies of the press release on the table and started for the kitchen. 'I'll attend to the forgotten flowers and other happenstance.'

'Wow. Mary. Wow. Mine's bigger than yours!' laughed Royal.

'Royal, we'd best read these quickly. Wow is right,' smiled Mary.

Media Press Release

Lakeville is the first city in Ontario, in the Earthen World, to host the Queen and King of Faery. To celebrate the 10th anniversary of The Annual Armour Street Barbecue, Queen

Titiana and King Oberon are the invited special guests,
inspiring this year's medieval theme. Mrs. Cravitz, the
Anniversary Coordinator from Armour Street, said in an
interview this morning that an Ambassador for the Little
People, Hector Grodstooth, is fielding questions from local
and global press from her residence. Ambassador
Grodstooth is a gnome and one of the signatories of The
Rekindlement Plan, as outlined below. The King and Queen
of Faery are pictured in the attached photograph and will
greet local dignitaries after the firework display this evening.
There will be announcements over the next several days for
citywide celebrations to be hosted by the Queen, King,
Ambassador and their people.

The Rekindlement Plan

1. *The People of Earth Meet The Little People of The*
   Under Earth
2. *World Leaders Gather*
3. *Local Sharing Gatherings Rekindling Friendships*
4. *Golden World Talks*
5. *Building of Heart to Heart Bridges*
6. *World Wide Celebrations TBA*

'Mary, you done?' asked Royal.

'Ya, just. What did Hector say about heart to heart
bridges?' asked Mary.

'I think he said the talismans will help us to build them,' said Royal.

'Too much, Royal. I'm in information overload. Hello up there Jesus. Please help me take in some more information because I think it's getting garbled,' said Mary.

'Double ditto babes. I think we should write some of this down before the party. He said some pretty heavy stuff and we should see what we remember now,' said Royal.

'What is a talisman? Isn't that something to ward off evil spirits?' said Mary.

'Evil spirits?' bellowed Hector from the kitchen. 'What are you Earthlings talking about now?'

'We're in information overload, Hector, and we were talking about the meaning of the word 'talisman'. Mary was thinking that it was something to protect us from evil spirits,' said Royal.

Hector walked in, almost stomping over to his chair and virtually flew to a seat beside Royal. He was standing atop the beautiful leather chair with his hands on his hips.

'Yes, Royal. A talisman may act as a charm to avert evil and bring good fortune, but the Queen of The Faery Talisman is something far more important. Your talismans hold faery dust, the kind that lasts for all eternity, and, when used properly, will produce magical marvels for all to see,' said Hector.

'Who was it that said, 'What's new is bright … and what's familiar is stale? I think we're being blinded by the light,' said Mary.

'Mary, you're a marvel. Now that you've had time to digest some of today's transpirations, I suggest you do just that, Royal, and write 'em down. Please allow me to suggest that you have your wishing well scribe or talisman scribe do the legwork for you. Know that all you must do is wish or desire an outcome, imagine it, and it will be created. Ah, there. I'm so good, I've done it for you,' said Hector as he pulled out two separate bindings, one with a cover inscribed with 'Royal Hickey's notes' and the other entitled 'Mary Hickey's notes' in fancy script.

'And please be aware that the press arrive at the Cravitz's in one hour. We should arrive earlier, only if to make Mrs. Cravitz more comfortable,' said Hector. 'I shall return in one half hour to escort you to the proceedings.'

Hector had arranged for the gnomes to watch over the children when they returned, with little doubt that they would be properly supervised considering the reprimands given out after the Tom in the Deeps incident. His gnomes were efficient and would take care of the flowers and any other matters of course that arose. He knew that Joan and Lucy had been visited by Ursula herself this morning and decided to ask Joan to join them at the press scrum so he wouldn't have to brief her later. It took some doing to convince Joan that Lucy would be in safe hands with Goddo, since she had learned of the incidents the day before. Hector persisted and Joan graciously agreed to join them. Hector suggested that he and Joan walk through the neighboring yards to the Kelly's home, mainly to encourage a familiarity with the other neighbors. Enroute, the odd looking couple were stopped repeatedly and asked about rumors. Joan matched Hector's finesse at diplomacy. She was a natural. Her next-door neighbor came running out the front door shouting when they were at his property's edge.

'Joan, Joan!' called the neighbor.

Joan turned and waved.

'Great to see you, Al. We're on our way to a press scrum to introduce Hector,' said Joan.

Al was out of breath by the time he caught up to them:

'Wait, wait! I haven't had the, uh, uh, pleasure, uh. Al Partridge at your

service, Ambassador. Mrs. Cravitz told me all about you,' said Al.

Hector blushed and held out his hand. Al was tall, at least six feet, and thought it was like shaking the hand of a small child. He adored children and wasn't the first earthling to mistake size for demeanor. Other neighbors, their 10 invitees, and staff hired as security or hospitality were out finishing off chores and setting up for the night. People saw

the commotion and were drawn to Hector's entourage. There must have been 20 people circling them by the time they arrived at the Kelly's. Mary and Royal noticed the growing crowd and came right out to join Hector. Although he never slowed, Hector was relieved to see Mary and Royal and kept up the pace, as he had several houses more before Mrs. Cravitz. His camaraderie was legendary amongst the little people, and Ambassador Hector lived up to his good name. By the time they arrived at the Cravitz residence, every person had been acknowledged and, more than that, felt honored to have met and befriended the Ambassador. Mrs. Cravitz, of course, had seen them coming and had opened her back garden gate for the arrival. Ironically, she admonished some of the nosier neighbors and demanded privacy and decorum. In no uncertain terms, Mrs. Cravitz held that there would be no lollygagging about in her yard.

As the five entered through her arched gate, Mrs. Cravitz smiled at the look of her garden. Hector had insisted on helping defray her costs, and had sent a troop over with new furnishings and gardening expertise. The results were fabulous. Cobalt blue morning glories against white trellises were the backdrop against her lovely white brick home. The orange tiger lilies towered above an explosion of red amaryllis to border giant yellow chrysanthemums and purple peonies. To her credit, Mrs. Cravitz had planted cedar hedges along the back and side property lines when she'd moved in all those decades ago. The cedars towered 40 feet, giving off an air of protection and privacy and were home to any number of species of her avian friends. Just off center of her yard, Mrs. Cravitz had a six by six foot pond with giant goldfish, lily pads and frogs. Hector's troop had arranged the wooden lawn furniture at center stage, with enough chairs to accommodate themselves and the seven invited press persons.

'Please sit down everyone. Abby will be out with refreshments shortly and the press should be here momentarily. The day begins!' said Mrs. Cravitz.

As she spoke, the tea service was brought outdoors with great fanfare. Mrs. Cravitz was explaining that the elaborate china set had been handed down to her on her mother's side and was hundreds of years old. The huge, round teapot was jet black and had room enough for over 40 cups of tea. Sunlight danced off the handle and top and it gleamed. The accompanying set had jet-black saucers lined on the inner and outer circles with gold. The cups were fluted and tall, with assorted yellow and pink roses painted in frames of gold on black.

'Exquisite!' said Joan as Mrs. Cravitz handed her a teacup. 'I've never seen a black tea set before.'

'Ah, the Queen herself would love to sit in this garden and sip from these, Mrs. Cravitz,' said Hector.

As Hector finished his sentence, a security guard peeked through the garden gate and asked if the press could enter. The moment had come.

The garden party went on for hours, with all participants oblivious to the growing party outside the gates. Hector enthralled the press and his friends with tales of long ago and talks of future. No one wanted the moment to end, but it was Hector that called for everyone to join the barbecue festivities.

'The dignitaries will be arriving soon; we must disperse and enjoy the festivities,' said Hector.

'But Ambassador, we have so many questions,' said a local newspaper reporter.

'Aye, I know. Too many! You must choose your first words carefully as I've written in the press release. All will flow and all will be well. We have the rest of our lives to work together and to answer questions, lass,' said Hector.

An explosion rocked the air. Hector flew straight up and stood solid on a large oak branch.

'Jigglypuff. Not to worry folks!' Hector called down. 'There's been a barbecue explosion and it looks like no one was injured; I shall return.'

With that, Hector flew over the top of the cedar hedge and disappeared from sight.

'Mr. Hickey, how did Hector fly? Mr. Hickey, what is going on?' asked a member of the press.

'Hold on! Hold on! Calm down,' said Royal.

Pandemonium erupted, but Royal's voice calmed everyone. Instantly, he took over and began talking about his family's experiences with Hector. Mary and Joan played along, knowing it would buy Hector time to get back and explain. In minutes, he returned, walking through the garden gate, but only to admonish his friends and the press. Shouting questions about the flying episode, Hector held up his arms to silence all.

'Folks! Everyone is fine, but we've lost one barbecue. Now, I said it was time to party. As to your questions, your theory of gravity isn't quite correct; there are three kinds, but I'll not be talking science with any of you tonight!' said Hector as he marched out the garden gate leaving a stunned group looking after him.

Hector was pleased. He had covered everything that the Queen and King had asked of him. The flying episode was a bonus. He thought it best to introduce a little of the fantastical before the Queen and King arrive. He had announced that their carriage would bring them to the Wee Lake gazebo in front of the Kelly's at 11:11 pm, only to meet a few select earthlings. The gazebo had been built in 1967 to commemorate Canada's Centennial and had been updated to its original splendor by a concerned citizen's group the

summer Joan and Lucy had moved onto Armour Street. Standing 50 feet tall, mainly to not block the view of the lake, the gazebo's roof was quite slanted and the columns were slender and fluted at the top and bottom. Sitting stage like about four feet off the ground, the 100 square yard surface was encircled by a short and wide fence carved with tulip pedestals that had been painted all the colors of the rainbow. Over the years, many people had enjoyed picnicking in gazebo shade or sitting on its bench-like fence. Tonight, international news was to be made in this most beautiful of settings. Filming of the event and photographs were welcome and encouraged. Hector had decided to mingle until then, mainly to offset any further incidents from disturbing the joyful atmosphere. He saw the Kelly children, John and Lucy checking out the tents near the lake, but he couldn't see Snelton or Granno, so he went to investigate. Mary and Joan caught up with him as he crossed the blocked off Armour Street and he noted that the bulk of the press continued to surround Royal on Mrs. Cravitz's side yard.

'Wow, Hector. That press announcement should get some attention,' said Mary.

'Just wait until they see the show tonight, Mary,' said Hector.

'What show? You mean when the King and Queen arrive?' asked Joan.

'Yes, my lady. Ah, there's Granno. Oh, and the others,' Hector said as he stopped.

He noticed some of the service staff near the children and could see why they weren't working. The gnomes had been showing off and all of the tent work was complete. Hector could tell their handiwork because the bar held dozens of bottles of alcohol as well as dozens of bottles of gnome water. He saw the Jack Daniels, Smirnoffs, Captain Morgans and such right beside the tiny but mighty Queen's Touch and King's Pail. The Mi'kmaq had called their drink 'firewater', but gnome water was its proper moniker. *Harmless fun. Hope not too many land dwellers drink gnome water tonight. Might prove even more entertaining than the Queen!* Hector's reverie was broken by a scream coming from near the Kelly's house. Hector was a blur and then gone. Joan and Mary started in that direction, yelling at the kids to stay put. Ignoring the warning, Lucy caught up and passed her Mom just as they entered her yard.

'*Was that a kid? It sounded like a kid,*' said Lucy in her head.

'No, I think…' started Joan as another even louder scream started on the other side of the house. As Lucy rounded the corner, she saw Hector taking a book, the biscuit colored book from her vision, from a young girl.

'It's okay, wee lass. She's gone and I won't let her back. There now. Ah, there's my little Lucy. Here you go, Lucy, take the book inside and I'll take the young lass to find her Mama,' said Hector.

'Elaine! Did Hector startle you? It's okay,' said Joan as she took the little girl's hand and turned to Hector. 'Elaine lives two doors down; I'll take her home.'

'It was that old lady who scared me. She kind of looked like you, Mrs. Kelly, but way, way older,' said Elaine. 'I wasn't afraid of you, Mister; you're cute. She said that I was to give the book to Lucy right away. She said I had to go near the lake, that Lucy was near the lake. I told her I'm not allowed...'

Elaine continued to talk while Joan directed her home and everyone else followed Lucy to the front door.

'For Ursula to act so rashly, something's up. I've got to get to the woods to contact her, but I must stay here until the arrival of the King and the Queen. Let's see if she's left a note or a clue in the book,' said Hector in his head to Lucy.

'Hector, there is just so much to take in. I've got enough to keep me reading for a long time and here Ursula wants me to do it right now?' said Lucy.

Hector retrieved the book from Lucy and set it on their dining room table. Mary had asked the others to stay outside, so it was only the three of them peering at the ancient cover. Mary let out an audible gasp.

'I know. I know. It's your pyramid and sphere,' said Hector.

'No, Hector. Well, that, too, but it's the title,' said Mary.

'You know the meaning?' asked Hector.

'I don't know what all the symbols mean, but I remember these words from high school Latin. It means *Peace On Earth*,' said Mary.

Chapter 15

Fireworks

Ursula enjoyed her few moments on solid ground. It had been a long time. Not knowing about the night's medieval theme, she was surprised when no one noticed her as she walked down Armour Street. *Especially since I was carrying the peace manuscript.* She well remembered the towns in Europe back in the 1500s. Everyone walked carefully down the muddy streets, avoiding the garbage people threw out of their homes, but they noticed everyone and everything. They were in survival mode. The smells came back to her. Foul odors from the open drains running alongside the streets. She favored the outskirts of the city, where she'd lived as a child in the cave with a clear stream running near. Why could she remember so vividly the details of a few moments in time, when most of the world had forgotten so much of their history? She knew the answer and she knew that what she was about to do was risky, but she had to return to Armour Street to feel comfortable that all was going as planned. She had waited for the sun to set and then had materialized inside the temporary festival compound. *Maybe I should have talked to Queen Titiana.* As she walked past the Kelly residence for the second time that day, she felt goose bumps or truth bumps, knowing that all was in perfect order. Five hundred years before, Ursula had felt that same absolute knowing. Smiling, she looked toward the gazebo and froze.

Had anyone seen her face at that precise moment, Armour Street residents would have heard a few more screams. And following her gaze would have seen a yellow haze near the stairwell of the gazebo. Earthlings may not have perceived the haze, but it was in plain sight to Ursula. Any haze portends a Formorian presence, but a yellow haze indicates a particularly nasty Formorian of the runners' tribe, and Ursula hadn't seen one in hundreds of years. The shift caused by her entry into the realm had formed a rift between worlds and danger was imminent. In a split second, Ursula had traversed the lawns and virtually cloaked the area containing the haze. Imperceptible to the human eye, a dance of death followed. On another level, Ursula was surrounded by several runners and wished she had paid more attention to her instincts and brought her wand.

While Ursula was fighting for her life, Hector left the Kelly's and headed toward the gazebo. He had some time before the Lakeville fireworks were set off and he wanted insure that all was in proper order. Lucy and Joan were scouring over the book, looking for a clue to decode its meaning. The three of them had tried to contact Ursula to finish off the conversation about unlocking the secret of the peace manuscript, to no avail. Hector told them not to dally too long, and to get outside to mingle. *'There's always tomorrow'*, he yelled back to them as he left for the gazebo. *The King and Queen will be delighted.*

In the darkened sky, the lighted gazebo looked every bit out of a fairy tale. Hector had cloaked himself in order to not attract a crowd and was at the gazebo in hyper speed. He noticed a blur of yellow to his right as he landed on the gazebo's top step and put it off to his slowing down to stop. He looked around at the white tulip double pedestal podium and smattering of chairs and smiled, proud of his accomplishments. *Everything is in perfect order.* As he thought the words, Hector became aware of the Queen's contact signal. He disappeared instantly.

'Hector. It's Ursula. She's gone,' said the Queen, sitting down on her chair, head held in her hands.

'Gone? What do you mean, 'gone'?' said Hector, reeling from the news.

'We were too late. She was so brave,' said the Queen.

'Please, tell me. What happened?' said Hector going down on his knees to comfort her.

'It was the runners, Hector,' said the King as he entered from the south wing door.
'Seven of them.'

Color drained from Hector's face as he remembered the yellow blur. He had never seen a creature from the runner tribe, but they were known as Yellow Death. Legend said that they stood about two feet tall with scaly skin the color of

238

ochre. Their bright yellow hair was almost fur like and covered their bodies in an hourglass shaped mane. Their strength was in their numbers, as they traveled in packs and overtook prey by sheer force. Over his 500 years on Earth, Hector had seen firsthand the effects of the concept of death on humankind and longed for the day he knew was coming when there would be no death, no anguish. But he couldn't understand about Ursula. She was of another realm where death did not exist. How could she be gone?

The King went on to tell Hector of the struggle. By the time they had arrived to help, five runners lay at Ursula's feet and the two standing were in rough shape. Just as the King and Queen materialized, the runner behind Ursula snapped his whip around her neck and took her out. The King defeated the last runner and turned to his Queen. They had to retreat to the Castle. In their long lives, they had known a few victims of the Yellow Death and none had ever returned from the Formorian stronghold. When the King had gone to retrieve the ancient Formorian artifacts hidden in their study, the Queen spoke Hector's name.

'I was there. I saw the yellow, but…' Hector started.

'Hector! Stop. You couldn't have known. It's been centuries, before you were born, since the Yellow Death have dared crossover. Ursula must have left a trail,' said the Queen.

'Ah. She showed herself this afternoon, bringing a book for Lucy Kelly,' said Hector.

'What book?' demanded the King.

'It's a very large, very old book with your symbols and the words *Peace On Earth* in Latin on the cover,' said Hector.

The King sat down.

'Ursula should have told us that she had it. We could have dealt with it together,' said the King.

'I think she was trying to protect us, Ob,' said the Queen.

'Yes, yes, but look what's happened now. She's caused a rift to form and we don't know the precise location,' said the King.

'I think I do,' said Hector.

Everyone jumped to their feet as the King shouted, 'Take us there immediately!'

It was 10 p.m. and the first firework had exploded over Wee Lake with a sonic boom. Hector and the King and Queen magically appeared on the gazebo as the crowds looked upward. Hector showed them where he had seen the yellow blur and the three jumped over the rail and stood on the ground where the battle had begun. Immediately the King shifted to his right.

'Excellent work, Hector. This is it. I have the seal,' said the King as he pulled a pouch out from beneath his

240

cloak. Had anyone looked at the three little people at that moment, they would have seen the King open the black velvet pouch and a stream of larger red rubies flow down to the earth and form a circle with a cross through. As if on fire, the rubies sank beneath the ground and the scorched grass returned to a healthy state. Nonchalantly, the trio sped through the crowd to the Hickey household.

After peering over the Peace On Earth manuscript with the children, Mary and Joan had decided to part ways and ready themselves for the festival. Mary and Royal were sitting in front of their home with some close friends and family members when the kids ran over announcing the fireworks were about to begin. They had been mingling with the neighbors and walking up and down the street for hours. As planned, they had regrouped around nine to enjoy a few cocktails before the big event. Everyone on the other side of the lake was thinking that the fireworks at 10 p.m. were the 'big event', but everyone at the barbecue anticipated the arrival of the King and Queen of Faery at 11:11 p.m.

As the Little People suspected, the Hickey's backyard was deserted during the firework display. The Queen called for her Lead Trooper and hordes of gnomes appeared instantly. She stood atop the Hickey's outdoor table and had the faeries sprinkle lights over the yard. Resplendent in her pink taffeta gown, the Queen commanded attention and got it. She warned her warriors to remain vigilant, as the

241

Formorians had shown on this side. She explained the situation and sent the cloaked gnomes out to their posts. The Lead Trooper remained with the King and Queen.

'Another 500 years and our dragons would have handled all of this, Titiana,' said the King.

'Aye, Obie. They'd probably give them a good run right now, too,' said Queen Titiana.

King Oberon raised an eyebrow. He wondered what his comrade from China, Emperor Myching, would have to say about that. Myching had been gifted with two of the baby dragons and had graciously shared with Oberon his knowledge of dragon history. Oberon was grateful for the sharings, as some knowledge was locked in his vaulted Halls. Oberon wasn't completely certain, but he thought that Merlin had hexed and locked some of the stones until future years. It was Rungdelf who had taught him about baby dragons all those centuries ago. Thousands of generations of dragon kind had come to an end with the death King Arthur's friend, Jee. Oberon had heard that the Lady of the Lake had tried to intervene at the final dragon battle. With his last breath, King Arthur threw his sword, Excalibur, into the lake. Jee had been mortally wounded only moments before and fell from the air, disappearing into the wake with Excalibur. The Lady of the Lake's banshee wail was heard over all the islands, sending shivers of fear through even the mightiest of men. That day, the Lady of the Lake had become the keeper of the sword and

Jee's kind had become extinct. Oberon knew that day as the end of an era, until Rungdelf showed up with his precious trunk. *I think Titiana's right about the baby dragon's being ready. I well remember the day that Rungdelf opened the trunk, smiling. I thought the stones were beautiful with all the vibrant colors and intricate markings. When he told me they were dragon eggs, I was flabbergasted. Merlin knew 'The Deeps' would be perfect for hatchlings and that I would create a dream world there for them to grow, safe from all harm.*

'Rungdelf did tell me that they're flourishing in the dream vault, Sir,' said his Lead Trooper, Mack Mackey.

'Mack. Wouldn't it be supersplendifous, as our Hector would say, to let the wee babies fight our battle? Aye, and they will someday, but not today. I must talk to Emperor Myching immediately. I shall return momentarily,' said King Oberon as he disappeared.

The Queen of Faery, Hector and Lead Trooper Mackey busily discussed strategy in somber tones under the faery lights in the Hickey back yard. Around the front of the house, there was an underlying current of excitement as the grand finale fireworks were done and the time moved closer to 11:11 p.m. At Lakeville's premier park, the festivals usually ended with the fireworks, so the crowds began to disperse after the grand finale. The park was on a point of land, jutting out into Wee Lake, with a marina overloaded with fenced off docks on one side and manicured rock and flower gardens sloping down to the lake on the other. Over 10,000 people could squeeze around the central stage in the middle of the park, but it took a little under 15 minutes to clear out the crowds. The Queen and King thought it best for the land dwellers to hear about Rekindlement Plan en masse from their nightly news on television, the Internet or from the newspapers the following day. Everyone at the Street Barbecue was privy to the 11:11 p.m. arrival time and eagerly anticipating meeting the King and Queen of Faery, but few others had heard of the Little People.

The King returned with dragon news and sent Hector and Mack out with the Troops. Hector noticed the thinning crowds across the lake and was grateful that the neighbors had vacated the gazebo. The Royal Carriage would be landing there within the hour and he and Mack had to secure the area. He was so distracted by thoughts of Ursula and the Formorian runners that he didn't notice Lucy running toward him.

'Hector, I know something is going on. What is going on?' said Lucy.

'Stop it, Lucy. You're attracting attention. Tonight is for the King and Queen of Faery. Tomorrow is soon enough for more stories, okay?' said Hector.

As they were speaking, Ruby Hickey ran across her lawn calling Lucy. Lucy looked hard at Hector and then turned away to smile at her friend.

"Coming, Ruby!" said Lucy.

Without looking back at Hector, Lucy spoke to him: '*Hector, please come first thing in the morning; there's something important I need to tell you.*'

Hector was relieved that Lucy would be busy with the other children and turned to see if Mack had any news to report. When the mightiest of the Troopers tipped his hat to Hector, a relief washed over him. *King Oberon has successfully kept the Formorians locked out. For now. Yes, Little Miss Lucy, I will be at your door first thing. The peace manuscript is the key.*

Hector felt secure with Mack and the boys at their stations and decided to carry on with his duties as Ambassador. He approached the first tent, asked for a wee dram and walked toward the Hickey residence with a broad smile. There were a dozen neighbors sitting around the lawn table, which Mary had asked Hector to decorate. The volume level was quite loud and it looked like a few in the party had tried the wee folk firepower. There were the usual chips, pretzels and miscellaneous spills on the table and more than a few empty drinking glasses. Since it was a free bar, the families chose to use reusable party cups to avoid glass breakage and such. Royal saw Hector coming and clapped his hands together for attention. The group had been discussing the significance of the time of arrival, 11:11 p.m. A numerologist had started the conversation noting that the number 11 represented heaven and 7 was the number of earth. One of the children insisted that wishes come true if you wish when you see two elevens together. With the noise at a dull roar, Royal used his amazing vocal chords and spoke above the crowd: 'Welcome, Ambassador Hector. Please join us as we have a seat of honor for you here.'

Hector smiled as he saw the chair, a product from the Wishing Well, he knew.

'Master Royal. You have outdone yourself. I shall be seated and have a wee sip with you before the Royal Carriage arrives,' said Hector.

Everyone laughed as Hector walked up and around the spiral staircase that was a part of the back of the chair and found himself seated at eye level with the other guests. The chair was a huge hit.

'Hector, we are about to commence the countdown to 11:11 p.m. Joan just ran inside to get the countdown clock,' said Mary.

As Joan came out of the house, Hector was thrilled to see another Wishing Well product. *Whoever said these folks didn't have imaginations hasn't seen them with a Wishing Well!*

'Bravo, bravo!' someone yelled.

'I love it!' yelled another neighbor.

Joan set the countdown clock on an easel at the end of one table. *Nine minutes. Oh my.*

Hector checked his time against the clock time and knew it was correct. But it was the elaborate likeness of the Queen and King that took his breath away. Mounted on the clock were the statues of the leaders of the Faery standing atop the Royal Carriage. One of the newspapers asked for everyone to gather around the clock for a group photo before leaving for the gazebo. Hector insisted on his chair being in the shot, with him on it. With their arms raised in a toast of friendship, the photographer snapped the picture and everyone cheered. As the photographer's flashpots of light were being dismantled, Hector and the guests spoke of moving over to the gazebo. The younger people had already started over when everyone noticed the light in the sky. On the other side of the lake, it looked like a spotlight was shining heavenward from the downtown core. Another light appeared. Both lights were white, like the airport beacons, swaying a little against the dark, cloudless sky. Within seconds, that entire side of the city was filled with lights, hundreds and hundreds. The white lights began to change to a myriad of colors and everyone watched as a light show of mythical proportions played out over Lakeville.

The Countdown Clock was long forgotten when a huge, white cloud appeared high above the earth, center sky.

The cloud was shaped like a bird, a hawk or an eagle, and then it began to dance. The crowd was mesmerized, everyone looking upward. Suddenly, the center of the cloud disappeared and there was a void, surrounded by the outline of the bird. Out of the center of the void, sprang the Royal Carriage of the King and Queen of Faery, led by their Royal Reindeer and surrounded by dozens of forest pixies. Resplendent in its glory, the Carriage reflected the beams of colored lights and left a trail of faery light dust falling gently over the land below. With a startling speed, the Carriage descended and swooped around Wee Lake once before gently landing at the gazebo. If anyone had cared to look, they would have seen the Countdown Clock reading 11:11 p.m.

Chapter 16

The Aftermath

Lucy woke with a start. Without moving, she glanced out her bedroom window and saw the sun beginning to rise in the sky. She looked at her Winnie the Pooh alarm clock, the only item on her nightstand. *10 o'clock. How did I sleep so long?* As she jumped out of bed, she called to her Mom.

'We're down here, Luce,' said her Mom. 'We were just going to wake you up.'

She called that she'd be down in a second and went into the bathroom. Lucy didn't have to ask her Mom who was there, because she knew Hector was as anxious as she about Ursula's book. She'd had another dream and was glad that he was there, thinking he could shed some light on what was happening to her. After the magical arrival of the King and Queen of Faery at 11:11 p.m., all of her neighbors, friends and press crowded around the gazebo. Intended to be a meet and greet for a few lucky people, the evening parlayed into an event of mythical proportions. The King and Queen of Faery wowed the crowd. Hector, Mack and the Troops joined in the fun and the people of the earth were left amazed.

I wonder if I had that dream because of all the fairy lights.
Lucy's mind drifted back to the night before, and
remembered the feeling when the Queen announced the faery
brigade. It was right after the welcoming committee finished
with the formalities. The Queen had been quite quiet
throughout the ceremony. She was exuding serenity and
obviously enjoyed watching her husband in the limelight. She
stood behind him half a step until the Mayor began to
applaud. Titiana stepped forward and held her husband's
hand and together they raised both arms high above their
heads. As the crowd quieted, the King and Queen called out
"Thank You" three times in succession. After the third
thanks, the Queen said, "And now, a few welcoming gifts,
dear friends!" With those words, there was an explosion of
color overhead and fairies began to fly out of the center, all in
a straight line. They all looked like variations of Trinity,
slender with long, lustrous hair and sparkle dresses of all
colors, leaving trails of faery dust as they went about a circle
above the crowd dispersing lights that glowed and floated in
mid air.

The faery dust was as thick as fog for a few moments
and as it dispersed, all of the people saw boxes and bags of
all sizes floating on parachutes and parasols down among the
crowds. No one could be hurt by the landing packages, as the
faery lights lit up the lawns like daylight and the presents
floated down in slow motion. The young children that had

managed to stay awake so late were instantly buzzed out of their tiredness and the older generation let any nagging concerns aside and enjoyed the moment.

Lucy picked up her hairbrush and noticed the faery box on her nightstand. As she brushed her hair, she flipped open the lid and her eyes widened in awe of the beautiful tiny harp sitting on folds of golden silk. She had tried to play it, but decided it was an ornamental harp to be admired for its beauty. She would treasure it always, a memento of the night the King and Queen of Faery entered her realm with great fanfare.

"Lucy!" called her Mom.

Startled out of her reverie, Lucy set the brush down, closed the lid on the harp and ran to the stairs. She could feel the warmth of the ruby stone in her pocket and slid her fingers into her jeans to pull it out. *Hector needs to know about the ruby stone right away!*

Meanwhile at the Hickey residence, Royal and Mary were sitting near the crabapple tree in their backyard enjoying reliving the wonders of the night before.

'Did you see Mack's face when he saw our necklaces, Royal?' said Mary.

'Did I? How could you miss it?' said Royal. "He's quite the character, eh, Mar?"

'Ah, we good folk know secrets beyond your human imaginings, Royal; and you'd be wise to remember not to wish too hard for something, or you just might get it.' Mary said as she mimicked Mack, the Lead Trooper. 'I wonder why they call them troopers anyway? Did you ask him?'

'No, I didn't ask him. He doesn't seem like the type that would answer too many questions. I did ask him what he knew about the talismans and he just gave me the runaround. Said he didn't know a thing about any pyramid or faery dust.' Royal said and smiled at Mary. 'You're right, he is a character.'

Mary then told Royal about a dream she'd had the night before. There were several people following Mack through desert sands when they arrived at the foot of the Sphinx. She hadn't seen the sphinx because it was night and she was focused on walking through the shifting sands. Mack stopped and asked everyone to wait. He stepped forward, out of sight, and everyone heard the grinding sound of stone on stone. A dazzling light lit up the darkness and Mack walked out of it toward them.

'Hmm. I don't get all this, Mary. I hope it's not too long before we figure out some stuff. I'm still stunned about our faery gifts from last night and now the dream,' said Royal.

Mary and Royal had been separated in the rush for picking faery gifts out of mid-air, with everyone vying for different boxes or bags. Mary's gift bag was a vivid golden color, flecked with gold dust and gold sequins. The matching parasol was standing in their front hall at this moment. Royal, on the other hand, had run after Angus, jokingly trying to grab a bag that had his son's attention. After missing Angus' bag, he turned back to the table as a shiny, navy blue box trimmed with fluorescent lilac ribbon was parachuted down before him. Royal was still laughing as he opened the box at the table.

Mary gasped and held up her gift. As far as they could see, everyone's gift was unique, but they had received identical and larger desktop versions of their necklaces in the very different packages.

'As long as we're enjoying the moment, Royal; the kids are having a blast and

I do have a good feeling about it all. It's been information overload, for sure; and something tells me that it'll keep coming fast and furious and that it's all good. I'm sure Hector or someone will eventually fill us in on the sphere-pyramid meaning,' said Mary.

They talked until the kids came down and then they talked their stories over again with the kids. The whole Hickey family went about enjoying the day in their newly decorated faery home with their faery presents in a new faery world.

'A ruby stone? Where did this come from, child?' said Hector.

Lucy told Hector how she'd held back information about Ursula's treasure box. There had been so much going on that she hadn't had time to digest all the new developments. There was the fact that her home and neighborhood was overrun by the faery folk, her ancestor had sent her a treasure trove that included The Book of Spells, the Diary, a crystal wand and a prophecy scroll. She hadn't noticed the secret compartment in the treasure box that held the ruby stone until she read about it in the secret compartment in the diary! Hector and Joan had been trying to decipher the Peace Book all morning, as they knew it had vital information because Ursula had risked everything to bring it to them. When Lucy held out the ruby stone, Hector recognized it as the seer stone from the Mi'kmaq years. He knew then that John and his grandmother Mickey needed to be there.

'Good work, Lucy,' said Hector. 'Please call John and tell him to come as soon as he can with his Grandmother. Tell him it is Official Faery Business. He'll understand.'

'OK, Hector. Should I get the Book of Spells and wand and stuff out, too?' said Lucy.

'Child. One thing at a time. They need to get here yesterday,' said Hector.

Soon after, the four people listened in awe as Hector gazed through the ruby stone and read from the Peace Book. Lucy asked if she could take notes, but Hector insisted that they all hear it together first to see what each could intuit about meanings. The ruby stone made the book come alive. Moving pictures, much like those seen on the ovals of the Halls, interspersed with the spoken word detailed the story of Godkind, womankind, mankind, faerykind, dragonkind, of all kinds, all grouped together on earth. Each time a picture came to life, Hector would patiently wait until all four had shared in its glory. Fascinated by the epic nature of the story, no one commented at all.

Chapter 17

The Final Frontier

It had been years since Hector had seen Zella. Too long. He smiled as he walked down the path toward her home. The smell of evergreen reminded him of his youth and Kaq and the long walks in the forest. He breathed deeply through his nose and obediently let the breath go out his mouth. Well taught and at such a young age. That Bezzy was something. He heard the rhythm of the woodpecker tapping away in the distance. He noticed the whistling cardinal and thought it quite close. He spied the garnet red flash and saw he had his little brown tinged partner flying close by. The brush began to thicken and soon the path was almost non-existent. Zella's touch was not lost on Hector. Where anyone else would notice no change in the peaceful forest, Zella's crystals and creations vibrated and rang clearly in his ears. This way. That way. Her directional clues were exactly like her singsong voice. *Ah.* He shivered.

Hector.

Did I hear something? Did someone say something?

It was the huge rose quartz crying out to him. He knew there was one about 20 feet ahead; he'd heard it for some time.

It isn't only the rose quartz. She's here watching me.

Hector stopped.

Christ to my left. Christ to my right.

A giggle above.

Yes, I heard you, Hector. About four miles ago.

Hector floated up to the limb of the old oak where Zella sat. Had that tree been there a moment ago? The question in his mind was gone before the thought finished. *Zella.* Looking resplendent in her silvery garb, he felt shivers in his calves as he neared her. To look at Zella was like looking upon the face of Love. Not many knew of her existence, as she wished, and she lived happily far in the forests of Shar. It was a rare treat for her to see the likes of Hector and she was relishing every nanosecond.

I see you haven't changed your dress in a few hundred years. Thanks be to the Creator.

Her 'dress' was as fine as any evening gown ever sewn, clinging to her curves as sunlight to glass. The last of her race of the mighty Tuatha Dé Danann, her height dwarfed Hector as he gazed upward in awe. Every nuance of her body glistened and gleamed. When she moved, Hector saw poetry in motion. The silvery sparkles were touched with a powdery blue tinge, which complemented Zella's long, auburn hair. Her sky blue eyes never left Hector.

Why have you been so long, Hector?

Ha. You know as well as I, Zella, that after the war, I have only been here a handful of times. No one in all Creation could gaze upon yoursElf for long. But now, since you were the only one of your race to survive the changes, you must rise and lead our forces.

She curled up her legs and rested her chin on her knees with a merry smile.

Hector, again everything is changing. I sense you're heralding in the Golden Age. Tell me your story, Hector. Tell me everything.

...to be continued

♥

WIN FREE COPY OF ZELLA!

Remember the seven baby dragons in the dungeon of the Faery King?

Here's your chance to win the second book in the series by naming one or more of the baby dragons…

~ Zella and The Little People ~

AND

have your name mentioned on my gratitude page… enter at:

www.MaryMcGillis.ca
or www.MaryMcGillis.com

31519940R00148